11·25·21

A Lass Resort

Gayle Roper

AnniesFiction.com

Books in the Scottish Bakehouse Mysteries series

. . . and more to come!

Library of Congress-in-Publication Data
A Lass Resort / by Gayle Roper
p. cm.
I. Title
               2021938780

AnniesFiction.com
(800) 282-6643
Scottish Bakehouse Mysteries™
Series Creator: Shari Lohner
Series Editor: Elizabeth Morrissey
Cover Illustrator: Kelley McMorris

10 11 12 13 14 | Printed in China | 9 8 7 6 5 4 3 2

Molly Ferris was completing a sale when the door of Bread on Arrival opened and three of the most extraordinary men she'd ever seen walked in from the cold December day.

She recognized them immediately.

The eldest, somewhere around fifty, had the craggy, handsome face of a man who had spent his life saving the world from evil cabals and treacherous regimes. The one in his midthirties had the sculpted abs and broad shoulders of kids' action figures the world over and the sweet smile of the boy next door, dimples and all. The youngest had the round cheeks and uncertain movements of an early teen but the unconscious charisma of someone who would one day become a magnet for adoration.

All had the most amazing blue eyes.

Molly's breath caught in her throat. She couldn't believe it. Superstar Adrian Sinclair, his equally well-known nephew, Rocky Sinclair, and some not-yet-famous young Sinclair had stepped into her Scottish bakehouse. Of all the bakeries in all the towns in all the world, they'd walked into hers.

Talking quietly together, they made their way to the display cases and began debating what they wanted to eat.

Molly blinked herself back to the real world. She grinned at her friend, police officer Greer Anderson, who stood waiting for her change for the melting moments she was buying.

"You do know that all their exploits are phony, right?" Greer muttered as she shot the trio a skeptical look. "It's the stuntmen and body doubles who do all the real work."

Molly raised an eyebrow. "And you know all this how?"

Greer shrugged. "I read."

"You're just afraid they're going to put the Loch Mallaig police department out of business as they fight for truth, justice, and the American way," Molly teased.

"I'm afraid they're going to give us more work than we need with their crazy parties and wild living."

"Really? Those guys?" Molly studied the Sinclair men. Adrian was pointing to a Scottish snowball, a sandwich cookie with raspberry filling and coconut coating. Rocky already held a prepacked box of shortbread, and the boy whose name Molly didn't know was asking bakehouse employee Bridget Ross for double cream cheese on his bagel. Somehow, the college-age girl was managing to serve them as if drop-dead gorgeous celebrities came into their Upper Michigan bakeshop every day.

Bridget glanced at Molly with an expression of wonder lighting her delicate features. When the men had their orders, she disappeared into the kitchen, doubtless to tell Laura Donovan and Carol MacCallan, Molly's friends and business partners, about their famous visitors.

Molly eyed the disgruntled Greer. "I don't see much about these guys in the tabloids."

Greer smirked. "Molly Ferris, a tabloid reader. Who'd have thought?"

"I check the headlines while I wait in the line at the supermarket," Molly corrected. "'Tragic last days of—' or 'Martian sighted in—,' or 'So-and-so has finally found true love.' I never see these guys' names. They seem to avoid the party circuit."

"There were pictures of Rocky all over the media last week. Each was with a different woman." Greer withdrew a melting moment from her bag and took a bite, a smile chasing away some of her grumpiness.

"He's got a new movie coming out, right? He was probably promoting it." As a former event planner now in charge of the bakehouse's marketing efforts, Molly knew a thing or two about the importance of promotions.

"Another Matt Bryant film." Greer rolled her eyes as if the character had offended her personally.

"I like Matt Bryant movies. Great action and intricate plots. I read Adrian played his father this time for comic effect."

Greer made a disgruntled noise.

Molly watched the men wander to a table and sit. "I wonder what they're doing here. Loch Mallaig is a far cry from Hollywood."

Greer pulled another melting moment from her bag. Her attitude mellowed as she ate it. "I'm sorry for being so grumpy. Personal issue."

Molly was instantly concerned for her friend. "Are you okay?"

Greer waved a dismissive hand. "Some guy won't leave me alone."

"Like a stalker? I'd say you ought to call the police, but . . ." Molly motioned to Greer's tidy uniform.

"Ha." Greer pulled a face. "It's nothing that serious. The guy simply doesn't understand the words 'I'm not interested.'"

Molly grinned, taking in Greer's sparkling hazel eyes, athletic physique, and wavy blonde hair, which was currently pulled into a neat bun. "You're pretty and powerful. It's hard to resist."

"If you say so. I wish he'd move on, though. It's an uncomfortable situation to say the least." Greer zipped her coat against the December cold and pulled on a department-issued, fur-lined cap to cover her ears. "Have you thought of closing early to beat the weather? This storm is going to be a doozy."

"I probably won't since I live upstairs, but the others will go home soon."

"The sooner the safer." Greer waved her bag of melting moments. "See you when I run out." The bakehouse's fresh Christmas wreath thumped gently against the front door as she pulled it shut behind her.

Molly surreptitiously observed the three handsome men now drinking coffee and enjoying their treats. The white lights twinkling on the Christmas tree beside them highlighted their distinctive features.

Adrian held out his Scottish snowball. "This is better than one I had in Glasgow," he said loudly enough for Molly to hear.

She grinned. Scottish snowballs were a Laura specialty, and the former NYC chef would be delighted to hear the praise. Was there a way to work it into an advertising line? *Adrian Sinclair says* . . .

The front door opened again, and Bobby Elder of Lochside Realty swept in on a burst of cold air. Molly eyed the heavy skies over his shoulder. Nasty. They'd start dropping their loads any second.

Bobby pulled off his knit cap and ran a hand through his flattened hair. "Was that Greer Anderson I saw driving off?"

"It was," Molly said.

"I should have been a few minutes earlier." He stared down the road in the direction Greer's cruiser had gone.

If Bobby was Greer's persistent suitor, Molly was afraid he didn't have a chance. Not that there was anything wrong with him. She liked the man in spite of his always-on salesman persona. It didn't matter whether he was trying to convince St. Andrew's Church to buy new chairs for the fellowship hall or the town to fill potholes more quickly or a prospective buyer that this particular house was the one. He couldn't help selling, though he seemed to have a good heart. He was a bit full of figure, but he was handsome in a comfortable, well-rounded way.

But as a match for Greer, who was fit, feisty, and full of life? Molly couldn't see it.

Bobby grinned at her. "I see my clients are here already."

She realized he meant the Sinclairs. "The Sinclairs are looking for real estate in Loch Mallaig?"

Bobby's eyes were bright with excitement. "Adrian wants a vacation home on the lake, and Rocky wants a year-round place for him and his brother, Trace."

"The boy is Rocky's brother?"

"That's right. Rocky is Trace's guardian. Their parents died several years ago in a car accident. Apparently Rocky wants to get the kid out of the Hollywood scene, save him from all the dangers lurking there."

"By living up here? We've got dangers too."

"That's right," Bobby agreed. "Bears. Nature. Bad weather. Overzealous Scotsmen in kilts and tams determined to cling to their ancestral legacies." He chuckled at his joke, which referred to the town's enthusiastic celebration of its Scottish heritage. "But those aren't the same threat as wild living."

"Still," Molly mused, "moving to Loch Mallaig seems a bit extreme to me."

"It's a wonderful plan to me." Bobby rubbed his hands together, dollar signs practically floating in the air before him.

Molly glanced out the window again at the heavy, dark clouds. "I think this storm is going to interfere with your plans, Bobby. From what I hear, we're going to get snowed in big time. You won't be able to get to the properties you want to show, especially the ones on the lake."

Bobby waved her concern aside. "It won't be that bad. You know how they hype things."

"And sometimes they're correct. I think this will be one of those times."

Even as she spoke, rain began to fall in a fine mist—the kind that froze as soon as it hit the earlier snows already on the cold ground.

"I'd better talk to my clients," Bobby said, alarm creeping into his tone. "We need to move while we still can."

Bridget passed Bobby as he walked to the table and she went to the counter. She grinned at Molly, her eyes sparkling. "Can you believe I get to be in the same room with two of the most handsome men on the planet and their understudy? So exciting . . . yet all I want to do is leave before the weather gets bad."

"I was about to shoo you out," Molly said. "Chances are good we won't be open for the next couple of days. I'll give you a call when things settle down."

Bridget hesitated. "How tacky would it be to ask for a picture with them? So I can prove to the kids at school that I really waited on them." She was working on her degree in forensic science at nearby Superior Bay College.

"May I have another of these Scottish snowballs?" Adrian called. "They are amazing."

"You bet, Mr. Sinclair." Bridget hurried behind the counter. As she set the treat on the table in front of him, Adrian smiled at her. "Why don't you get your friend to take our picture?"

Bridget flushed and sent Molly a wide-eyed look. Molly whipped out her phone and snapped a photo. Bridget's smile lit up the room.

Bobby, who had stepped out of the frame, returned to the table. "We really need to get moving if we want to see some properties before the storm hits," he told his clients.

"First things first." Adrian took a bite of his snowball, raspberry jam oozing comfortably between the layers of cookie.

"I don't think we're going to beat the storm." Rocky pointed out the window. "It's already started. We should probably go back to Castleglen and hunker down for the duration. We can check out houses afterward. There's no hurry."

"If that's what you think is best," Bobby said, clearly trying to tamp down his disappointment. "I'm available whenever you are."

Adrian fixed his bright blue eyes on Molly. "You must know the weather up here. What do you think? Should we go back?"

"Returning to Castleglen is your safest option," she said. "It's going to be a very nasty storm. A cold front coming down from Alberta, Canada, and one coming up from Colorado are meeting here. Lucky us. It's beginning as rain, which will freeze on the cold ground and the snow we already have. When the temperature drops as the day moves toward night, the rain will give way to snow, dumping a couple days' worth on top of the ice."

"Do you get storms like these often?" Trace watched the threatening sky with an uncertain expression.

Molly wondered if the kid had ever seen a snowstorm of any significance. Southern California got heavy rains that led to mudslides, as well as earthquakes and terrible fires. Nothing to sneeze at there, but a whiteout blizzard was another experience entirely.

She smiled at the boy. "Fortunately we don't get storms of this intensity often. Lots of snow and cold, sure. It is the Upper Peninsula of Michigan after all. But we're all used to regular winter weather. You'll be fine at Castleglen." She appraised the men. "I do have to tell you that what concerns me most is your clothes."

All three men glanced down at their trendy jackets. In contrast, Bobby wore a beige puffy jacket that made him resemble a slightly toasted marshmallow. Not a particularly stylish sight, but a fully appropriate one.

"What's wrong with our clothes?" Trace asked.

"I'm sure in California, nothing," Molly answered. "But those jackets are not going to withstand a winter storm. Where are your hats and gloves? Your boots? Scarves?"

"Then we'd better get back to Castleglen." Rocky stood.

"May I recommend a stop at Northern Woods Outfitters on your way?" Molly suggested. "Our friend Trent McKade will get you dressed for the weather. Even after the storm's over, it'll still be brutally cold."

Bobby shifted nervously from foot to foot as if concerned that Molly's warnings might incite the men to flee Loch Mallaig, costing him his potentially lucrative sales. He stepped forward. "I can take you to Northern Woods, gentlemen."

Molly had to admire Bobby's moxie, a true salesman keeping himself front and center in the Sinclairs' minds.

As the men moved toward the door, it opened and several new customers blew in, including Fergus MacGregor, owner of Castleglen and Molly's beau. The other newcomers, two men and a young woman, seemed to know the Sinclairs, and loud chatter erupted as they greeted each other.

Fergus extricated himself from the crowd and moved to Molly's side. He had a smile just for her, and her heart did its usual jump of pleasure at seeing him.

"Is Neil at Castleglen holding down the fort?" she asked. Fergus's son, Neil, was his right-hand man at the resort.

"He's out of town at a hospitality conference," Fergus answered. "It's sunny and warm where he is, lucky man."

"That is lucky." Molly smiled brightly and nudged Fergus. "Though I prefer to be wherever you are."

"Or wherever Adrian and Rocky Sinclair are?" His silver-shot beard and mustache twitched with a teasing grin.

"They've got nothing on you," she said affectionately, meaning it.

That smile came again as he pulled off his knit cap and shook it, sending little droplets of rain flying.

She wiped a drop from her cheek. "It's getting worse out there, isn't it?"

"And will be a lot worse before it's over." His smile faded to concern. "Will you come stay at Castleglen for the duration? I don't like the idea of you alone in your little apartment upstairs."

Molly hadn't been looking forward to staying alone either. "I was thinking of asking Laura if Angus and I could stay with her." Her little Scottie wouldn't mind where he weathered the storm as long as he was with Molly.

"That's better than either of you being alone, but better still, why doesn't she come to Castleglen too? It'll be safer for her there. Her little cottage will get a lot of fierce wind and drifted snow since it's right on the lake."

Molly raised an eyebrow at him. "And it wouldn't hurt to have a gourmet chef on hand for your VIP guests."

Fergus blinked. "Do you really think she'd cook for us?"

"I'm sure she'd be delighted, especially if it means she gets to stay in one of those newly renovated rooms. I showed her pictures last week and her jaw dropped."

"I'll ask Trent if he'd like a room too." Fergus grinned. "Can't let a man be snowed in alone."

Molly chuckled. "Laura and Trent always have difficulty making their schedules work for dates. Being stranded together at Castleglen will certainly help."

"And I'll ask Carol and Harvey too. Their place is a bit isolated."

"Will it be a problem to host so many of us?" Molly asked, not wanting to impose.

"Not at all," Fergus reassured her. "These folks are the only guests I have left at the resort. When the forecast got dire, everyone decided they didn't want to get caught in the back of beyond for several days, and they left early. Incoming guests have decided to wait until after the storm. I can't give rooms away."

"Except to us."

He grabbed her hand. "There's no one I'd rather have with me."

Warmth slid through Molly at the affection in his blue eyes. He gave her hand a squeeze and released his grip, becoming all business.

"I've sent my staff home," he said. "Before the chef left, he prepared meals for the Sinclairs and me. Then this trio showed up." He indicated the folks he'd entered alongside. "The lone staff person still at Castleglen is the gym manager, Chet, who has an appointment with Rocky and wanted to wait for him. If anyone else wanders in needing shelter, Chet can take care of them until I get back."

"Hey, Fergus." Adrian waved a hand, indicating the chic woman, an older man wearing a golf shirt, and a muscular man in trendy clothing. "Come meet some business friends of ours."

"Be right there, Adrian." Fergus returned his gaze to Molly. "So you'll come to Castleglen, Molly?"

"I'll double-check with Laura and Carol, but I think you've got yourself a kitchen crew."

"Your safety is what's most important, but I'll take the kitchen help too." Fergus gave her a quick hug, then joined Adrian and his group.

"You got room for three more at that little place of yours, Fergus?" Adrian asked.

"All taken care of, Adrian," Fergus said. "I checked them into their rooms before we came to meet you. They're down the hall from you."

With a grin Molly headed for the kitchen and her friends. She knew they wouldn't mind cooking for everyone, especially since it meant enjoying the decadent luxuries at Castleglen. She felt a little bubble of excitement. What she'd thought would be a dark and lonely time, snowbound with her dog, now promised to be like a fun week at camp. She couldn't wait.

2

"Harvey's over the moon." Carol returned her phone to her pocket with a smile. "He's going to settle the girls in the garage. You know how he dotes on those hens."

Laura set a mixing bowl in the dishwasher. "Chickens in the garage?"

Carol shrugged. "It's better than putting them in the living room."

"I have to agree with that." Laura grabbed a dish towel and dried her hands.

Molly watched her friends with affection. Their friendship, sparked as college roommates, had weathered three decades of living states apart—Molly in Chicago, Laura in New York City, and Carol in Pittsburgh—and proven a strong foundation on which to build their business after they'd decided to reinvent themselves as bakehouse owners in the Upper Peninsula.

"It's more secure than their coop," Carol explained. "Winds could harm that structure, and airborne debris could damage it. The garage is dry and holds a temperature of about fifty, so they're safe there. Even if the electricity goes and we lose heat, it's warmer than the coop. Add lots of feed and water, and they're fine in the garage if we leave them for a few days."

"Won't they get frustrated pecking at that cement floor?" Laura asked.

"They'll find a roosting spot on a shelf or in a rafter and sleep most of the time," Carol said.

"And Pascal?" Molly rarely saw Carol's all-but-invisible cat, who loved hiding under beds.

"Jenny and Craig took him to their house. Searching for him will entertain Maisie and Gavin while they're snowbound." Carol grinned. "Should I feel guilty for spending the blizzard at a luxury resort while my daughter tries to keep up with twin seven-year-olds?"

"Not in the least," Laura said as she hung the towel to dry. "It was so generous of Fergus to invite us to stay at the resort. A major winter storm alone can be scary, especially if the electricity goes out." She had survived life in New York City, but the coming storm was scary in its own way. "As soon as I clean up things here, I'm there."

"Trent's invited too." Molly gave Laura a knowing smile.

Laura colored. "That's nice."

Molly suppressed the urge to roll her eyes. She'd seen the sparks flying between her friend and Trent, and she was glad Laura had found such a nice guy—even if she wasn't willing to call him her significant other yet.

Molly went back up front to tell Fergus that Carol and Laura were in, but she found chaos, with almost everyone speaking at once. The young woman who had entered with Fergus—a tall, elegant brunette with lots of long, sleek hair cascading down her back—currently wore a worried expression and paced by the door, talking on her phone. She wore a billowy red top over turquoise-and-red snakeskin leggings. Her white, knee-length cardigan would offer very little protection against the cold. Molly tried to decide if she should recognize the woman from some movie or show, but nothing struck her. Surely if she'd seen that gorgeous face on a screen, she'd remember.

A muscular man who bore a strong resemblance to Rocky stood off to the side chatting on his own phone. He seemed quite concerned about whatever was being said. Molly assumed he was Rocky's body double or stuntman. Suddenly he smiled, and he had his own charm.

Fergus was in deep conversation with Adrian, both of them laughing like old friends recalling old adventures. Had they known each other before Adrian had come to stay at Castleglen? She'd never heard Fergus talk about Adrian. Of course, Fergus hosted lots of notable guests at Castleglen, and he didn't go around bragging about them.

A man with an air of self-importance gesticulated wildly during what appeared to be a serious conversation with Rocky. His carefully barbered white hair was unaffected by the wind that had blown him into the bakery, and his strident voice carried across the room. "You can't do this, Rocky," he was saying. "You owe me."

Rocky shrugged, unmoved by the man's urgency. "I've more than repaid you for anything I might owe, Jonathan. You aren't my primary responsibility. I have to do what I think is best." What that responsibility was became obvious when his eyes cut to his little brother.

Trace stood uncertainly by the display case, shifting from foot to foot, appearing overwhelmed by all the noise around him.

Molly felt sorry for the boy and approached him. He glanced down at her, then away. She realized he was already several inches taller than her five-foot-four, well on his way to being the height of his uncle and brother. She smiled at him and waved her hand at the crowd. "Do you know who all these people are?"

He turned red at the attention. "Sort of."

When he said no more, she prompted, "Tell me, will you?"

"Um, sure. That big guy is Adam Lorbetski." He indicated the not-quite Rocky. "He's my brother's double."

Molly thought of Greer's comments. "That means he does all Rocky's stunts?"

Trace frowned. "Actually, Rocky does lots of his own stuff. He'd do it all if they'd let him."

Molly was touched by the boy's immediate defense of his brother.

"They're afraid he'll get hurt, you know, if they let him do it all," Trace continued. "Then production would be closed down and it'd cost everybody a lot of money. So they make sure Adam does the really dangerous stuff. He also does all the boring stuff, like blocking and the over-the-shoulder and distance shots."

"So he's important."

"Yeah," Trace said. "And he's nice. Rocky likes him."

As if he knew they were talking about him, Adam grinned at Trace and gave him a wink. Trace smiled back.

Molly followed the interaction. "You like him too."

"He's real."

And doesn't that say a lot about the others, Molly thought.

Adam lowered his head and, phone still to his ear, frowned again at whatever was being said on the other end of the line.

"His girlfriend has an ex who sometimes bothers her," Trace told Molly. "Maybe she's being hassled now that Adam's out of town. The guy hates Adam. He says it's his fault she broke up with him—which is ridiculous because Adam has only been with Jill six months. He didn't know her when she was with that guy."

"Sounds complicated," Molly said.

Trace shrugged. "Or maybe he's talking to the police. Some guy was trying to blackmail him, and he went to the cops about it. Now the guy's in trouble and is really mad at Adam."

"Well, he certainly has an exciting life. Who's the tall, pretty lady?"

Trace shook his head. "I don't really know her. She's Paula Somebody from the studio. She's here to get Uncle Adrian or Rocky to do something they don't want to do."

Molly watched Paula move back and forth as she continued to talk on the phone. She thought the woman appeared a little desperate.

Trace felt no such sympathy. "Good luck to her. Uncle Adrian and Rocky told everybody they would be unavailable. They didn't say why, but they made it clear they didn't want to hear from anyone from the studio or their agency about anything until the New Year."

Molly blinked. "Are you spending Christmas in Loch Mallaig?"

Trace shrugged. "I don't know. I guess it depends on whether Rocky or Uncle Adrian find some property they like."

"So you guys could become regular customers here," Molly said with a smile.

"They're determined to move to the area to 'save me from a life of corruption.'" Trace spoke as if he couldn't imagine such a life or understand why they thought he'd pursue it.

"We aren't exactly known for wild living in Loch Mallaig," Molly said. "How do they even know about this town? We don't get many celebrities."

"Uncle A knows the guy who owns the hotel where we're staying. They've been friends since forever."

"Your Uncle Adrian is friends with Fergus?" Molly wanted to hear that story.

"They went to camp together or something when they were young. When Rocky decided to get out of SoCal, Uncle A told him all about this place. So here we are, though I think they could have found a warmer spot." He glowered out the window. "Or at least waited until after the storm."

"Loch Mallaig isn't your first choice," Molly said sympathetically.

"Maybe a visit in the summer would be okay. But now? And to live here?" Trace sighed. "Not that anyone has asked my opinion."

Molly bit back a smile at the familiar lament, which she had heard from her own now-grown daughter, Chloe, on numerous occasions. She shifted her attention back to the people milling around. "Who's the man in the golf shirt, the one with the white hair?" She cringed inwardly at the shirt's thin cotton—not a good choice for Loch Mallaig in winter.

"Um, that's Jonathan Hooper." Trace said it as if Molly should recognize the name.

She shook her head. "I don't know him."

"He's head of The Hooper Agency." Trace seemed unable to fathom that Molly had never heard of the man.

"And what does The Hooper Agency do?"

"Mr. Hooper is the agent for some of the biggest names in Hollywood. He's Uncle A's agent and Rocky's. He says he wants to be mine."

"Are you going to carry on the family tradition and be an actor too?"

Horror flashed over Trace's features. "Not in a million years."

"What do you want to do?"

"I want to be a Marine." He blushed as if regretting what he'd said. "Forget it. It's a dumb idea."

"I don't think it's dumb at all. I think it's brave."

"Really?"

"Really." He wanted to be in real life what his uncle and brother were on the screen—a hero.

Adrian interrupted their conversation with his commanding voice. "She says we need better clothes for the weather." He gestured to Molly, and she stood straight at the sudden attention of everyone in the room.

"She's right." Fergus indicated Adam and Jonathan. "Sweatshirts and polos aren't going to cut it."

"Hey, I've got flannel on under my sweatshirt," Adam said in friendly self-defense as he slid his phone into his pocket.

Bobby raised his hand. "I was about to show them the way to the outfitters."

"Sounds good." Adrian started for the door. "Let's go, everyone. Puffy coats all around. And gloves and hats and boots."

"I've got boots." Paula, the woman Trace said came from the studio, held out a foot shod in a gorgeous turquoise cowboy boot, tooled and patterned and one of the most beautiful pieces of workmanship Molly had ever seen. It must have cost a fortune.

Adrian eyed the boots. "I don't think they'll cut it in this weather."

Paula's face fell at the lack of appreciation for her footwear. Adrian didn't notice as he and the others made for the door.

Molly approached Paula. "Your boots are absolutely amazing."

Paula perked up. "They should be for what they cost."

"I bet they're just the thing for home," Molly said, "but wearing them in this storm would be a crime. They'd be ruined."

"They can take a little rain." Paula indicated the outside.

"But what about ice and snow?" Molly asked. "Those slick soles will give you trouble too. Don't risk it. Here, you dress for the weather, not fashion. Forget looking good and choose safety—for yourself and those wonderful boots."

To help make Molly's point, sleet began tapping against the side window. Paula wound a strand of hair around her finger and studied first her boots, then Molly's practical, comfortable shoes. She eyed the nasty precipitation and shrugged in resignation. "I suppose you're right."

Molly peered out the side window to see how the parking area was faring. A human-shaped shadow interfered, briefly blocking her view of the rain and sleet. She blinked, the shadow disappeared, and she saw the parking area was still fairly clear of ice.

While Fergus remained inside to finalize plans with Laura and Carol, Molly followed the Hollywood folks to the front door and out onto the wraparound porch of the big yellow Victorian that housed Bread on Arrival. Wind blowing off the lake and through Dumfries Park drove the sleet sideways, but the deep porch roof offered protection. She pulled her sweater tight and folded her arms to hold in what body heat she could.

As people ran to their cars, they held up their arms for some protection from the icy needles. Paula slipped at one point, the slick soles of her cowboy boots no help at all. Molly worried she might fall, but she caught herself. At least she now hopefully understood the need for appropriate gear.

One by one the cars left the lot, all heading for Northern Woods Outfitters. In no time, Fergus's Range Rover and a gray SUV remained.

Molly was about to return to the warmth of the bakehouse when a short, slight figure raced from the back of the house across the parking lot. He wasn't one of those who had been in the bakery. He had a bulky backpack slung over one shoulder. He continuously cast about as though he feared being seen. He reached the gray SUV and opened the door, then carefully put his backpack inside. After one last peek around, he climbed in and left, heading in the same direction as the others.

Where had he come from? Curious, Molly made her way to the bend in the porch and gazed toward Dumfries Park. Had the man used their lot for his car, then gone to the park on foot? In this weather? In those inadequate clothes?

She glanced at the outside stairs that led up to her apartment. Perhaps he was a courier and he'd been upstairs searching for her. But if so, why hadn't he simply come into the bakehouse?

A gust of wind blew a fresh pulse of sleet across the porch and into Molly's face. She shivered, and suddenly it didn't matter where the man had come from, where he'd been, or where he was going. She was freezing. She hurried inside, pushing the door shut against the increasing wind.

Fergus came out of the kitchen and smiled that wonderful smile he saved for her alone. "I'm glad Laura and Carol are coming to Castleglen. We thought it would be best if I drive the three of you to the resort. Harvey will meet us there, as will Trent."

"That's very considerate," Molly said. "Your car is certainly better in these conditions than mine." She thought of the Range Rover's leather seats, which were butter-soft and heated. "And much more comfortable."

He touched his index finger to her chin. "Only the best for you."

She knew she was smiling like an idiot, but having someone who wanted to take care of her filled her with delight after all the years of having to rely completely on herself. She'd been lonely after her late husband had passed away more than a dozen years earlier, and she hadn't thought she'd ever feel this happy again. The affection of a good man like Fergus was rare, indeed.

Any thought of the furtive little man and his gray SUV disappeared into the sleet.

3

While Laura and Carol closed the bakehouse kitchen, Molly packaged all the food in the display cases for transport to Castleglen. Along with several loaves of bread, bagels, scones, cinnamon buns, and assorted cookies, there were half a dozen more Scottish snowballs that Adrian might enjoy over the next few days. Too bad Greer wasn't among the party, Molly thought wryly as she packed the remaining melting moments.

She left Fergus loading food into his car and raced upstairs. Angus sat on the bed and watched her place clothes and toiletries in her suitcase. His bushy eyebrows were pulled together in a worried expression.

"It's okay, sweet boy. You're coming along." She gave him an ear rub. He jumped from the bed, grabbed Woolie the sheep, his favorite toy, and sat beside the door. She smiled at him and reminded herself she needed to bring enough food for him to last several days. Who knew how long they'd be snowed in?

Fergus appeared to carry her suitcase and Angus's supplies, including Woolie, to the car. She donned her thick winter coat, scarf, hat, and boots, and followed him outside. She picked up Angus, who was already trembling inside his plaid coat, and hurried to the car, where Laura and Carol already waited. She grinned as she realized her friends had saved her the passenger seat. She slid in next to Fergus.

Angus cuddled in Molly's arms as they drove first to Laura's cottage for her to grab her belongings, then to Castleglen. The wind blew off the lake and peppered the car with sleet. The large SUV slid a little on the ice, and Molly was glad she wasn't driving.

When they pulled under the canopy before the resort's massive front door, she sagged against the seat in relief. The huge building protected them as they unloaded. In the adjacent parking lot, she spotted the vehicles of those who had been at Bread on Arrival earlier. Everyone had made it safely from Northern Woods Outfitters—including its owner, Trent, who was waiting for them in the lobby. He and Harvey discussed fishing animatedly, and Molly was almost surprised not to see any of Harvey's ice-fishing gear among the luggage he'd brought for himself and Carol. The California people had already gone to their rooms.

At the unmanned registration desk, Fergus gave everyone the key cards to their rooms. Molly set Angus down, pulled off her gloves, and took her key. She surveyed the vast lobby, which was decorated for the holidays with a bounty of fresh pine trees, boughs, and garlands wrapped in white lights and plaid bows. The space was usually teeming with people, but now it held only the six of them.

Fergus led them to the elevators and up to the second floor. The doors opened onto a long hall. "When you're settled, come downstairs to the den near my office," he said. "It's got seating for everyone and a large fireplace. The California folks will be coming too, and we can set up a general schedule for things like meals."

Molly noted that their little group was in four rooms in a row just past the stairs, first her, then Laura, then Carol and Harvey, then Trent. She suddenly wondered about Fergus. She laid a hand on his arm. "You're not driving to your house, are you?"

He shook his head. "I'm here for the duration. I've got the room across the hall."

"We want to thank you for having us, Fergus," Harvey said, his arm wrapped around Carol's shoulders.

Carol chimed in agreement. "We appreciate your hospitality."

"Absolutely." Laura used her key card and wheeled her suitcase over to hold the door open. "Staying here with friends is so much better than being in my little cottage alone."

Angus gave a little bark as if to express his thanks too, though Molly suspected he was also reminding them that they were indoors now and she could take his coat off.

"Glad I could help. See you in a little while." With a wave, Fergus disappeared toward the elevators.

Molly walked into her room, number 202, and the wall of windows on the far side immediately drew her. She crossed the plush, sage-green carpet to gaze out over acres of fairways and greens, roughs and sand traps, all buried under snow and the developing crust of ice. Beyond the golf course, the loch stretched into the distance. What would be a world of green and blue in warmer weather was shades of gray today—the deep gray of the roiling clouds, the soft gray of the biting sleet, the pocked gray of the icy snow-coated ground, the frosty gray of the lake disappearing into the mist.

She pivoted from the weather pinging against the windows to admire her opulent room. "It's been redecorated, Angus. Isn't it lovely?"

He barked agreement, and she bent to undo his coat. He went on his own explorations while she paused to revel in the wonderful results of the room's renovation.

She found the color scheme of toast, soft sage green, and cream chic and soothing. A king-size bed dominated the room, its crisp white linens and quilt topped with decorative pillows and a patterned runner that matched the drapes. A plump couch that was undoubtedly a pullout bed rested against one wall opposite a comfy chair and a desk holding a lamp bristling with plug and Internet connections.

She dropped into the overstuffed sage chair by the window and put her feet on the ottoman. "What do you think, Angus? Are you as impressed as I am?"

In answer, he jumped into her lap and rested against her with a sigh of contentment.

She leaned her head against the chair's back and smiled. For the next few days, she was a princess in a castle—when she wasn't the scullery maid cleaning pots after each meal, of course.

She rose, set Angus on the floor, and retrieved his dog dishes from their luggage. She went to fill a bowl of water for him. The bathroom's renovation matched the indulgence of the rest of the room. A double vanity was loaded with fragrant soaps and creams. A spa tub promised a relaxing soak, and the glass-enclosed steam shower was roomy enough for a small army. Towels that could wrap around her twice hung beside a thick, soft terry-cloth robe with a hood.

There was knock on the door. She opened it, and Laura sailed in. She greeted Angus, who brought her Woolie as a welcome present. She flopped down in the chair Molly had vacated. "I bet the Sinclairs have luxury suites, but I'm having a hard time imagining how they could be better than this."

Molly laughed. "In your wildest dreams, would you have imagined being snowed in with Adrian and Rocky Sinclair? I can't wait to tell Chloe." Her daughter was a veterinarian who lived and worked in Milwaukee. "She'll be so jealous."

"And you said they want to move to Loch Mallaig?"

Molly climbed on the bed and propped herself against the mountain of pillows. "That's the story according to Bobby Elder. He's going to sell them property. He hopes."

"Why here?"

"Trace says they want to save him from Hollywood."

"Does he want to be saved?"

"Good question. He's not happy about the move or the weather. He'd rather go somewhere warm."

"That shows the kid is smart," Laura joked. "I mean, I can understand if they want a summer place on Loch Mallaig—lots of people do—but isn't living up here full time a bit extreme, especially since their careers are based out of California?"

"Exactly what I've been thinking," Molly agreed. "It's not exactly commuting distance to Hollywood, even with a private plane."

"Well, they're going to get a big dose of winter in the next couple of days. It'll either break their resolve or make real Yoopers out of them." Laura checked her watch. "It's a little after three. Let's go downstairs to Fergus's den, then find the kitchen and see what we've got to work with. Hopefully the kitchen staff stocked up on supplies before Fergus sent them home to their families."

Leaving Angus behind to nap since they planned to be working in the kitchen, they collected Trent, Carol, and Harvey, then took the elevator down to the lobby. They started across the large open area where upscale lodge style was the order of the day—vaulted ceilings, massive rustic wooden columns, and clusters of comfy leather furniture. One wall was glass with a view over the beautiful grounds and golf course. Another was lined with the crests of various Scots clans, the lion rampant of Scotland itself in the center.

Because of the season, a large Christmas tree that dwarfed several others sat in the middle of the lobby, all balls and bows and bright fairy lights. Beautifully wrapped packages sat beneath it.

Past the registration desk, draped with evergreen swags, was a broad corridor that eventually led to Fergus's office. On their way down the hall, they passed the doors to the resort's two restaurants, both closed, the rooms dark. Usually Tee for Two, the breakfast and lunch bistro, spilled cheer and laughter from its bright interior, and King's Heid Pub filled the place with wonderful aromas and well-dressed diners. Both eateries provided views over the golf course and the lake. It felt strange to see the spaces empty and forsaken.

Across the hall from Tee for Two was the gift shop where guests could buy everything from toothpaste to a new dress or a handsome kilt. It too was dark. After the shop came restrooms, a series of meeting rooms, and a good-size ballroom with a grand piano nestled into an alcove outside. Fergus's office was beyond that, past the den they were heading for.

On the same side of the hall as the restaurants was the gym and weight room, its door wide, its light burning brightly. Molly had never had occasion to be in the gym, so she poked her head inside the door to check it out.

Laura paused beside her.

"Wow, this is quite the facility," Molly said, not that she was surprised.

"Only the best for Fergus." Laura elbowed Molly. "In all things."

Molly made believe she wasn't blushing as she took in the large room, part of it boasting a basketball court with a small set of bleachers along one side. Beyond the court was an exercise area full of top-of-the-line equipment and weights.

"There's a local league that plays basketball here as well as a church league." Trent pointed to a spot halfway down the court. "That's where the guy from Houghton stole the ball from me and scored the winning basket in the last second. Still hurts to think about it."

Laura laughed at his woebegone expression. "And when did this atrocity happen?"

"Last week," he said forlornly.

"Poor guy." Laura patted his back in comfort.

Voices sounded in the main hall, catching everyone's attention.

Rocky Sinclair and Adam Lorbetski emerged from a room farther down the hall. They were so deep in conversation they didn't see Molly and the others grouped around the gym door.

"At least I don't have to worry about Lou Duckworth up here." Rocky was handsome in a crimson sweater.

Adam, still wearing his plaid flannel and sweatshirt, appeared unconvinced. "You think a major weather system will keep him away from you? I don't think so. You're his meal ticket."

"No one knows where we are, including him."

"No one except everyone at The Hooper Agency and everyone at the studio."

Rocky mulled it over, then shook his head. "All they know is that I'm not available until after the New Year. They don't know where I am."

Adam pulled a face and drawled, "Jonathan Hooper and Paula What's-Her-Name. Enough said." Rocky groaned, and Adam laughed. "Ah, fame."

"It's not all it's cracked up to be," Rocky grumbled.

"It does have its downsides. I think getting that restraining order against Duckworth was smart."

"As if that will keep his long camera lenses from finding me." Rocky shook his head. "And people don't understand why I want to move some place without people like him."

Molly thought about Loch Mallaig. Once the locals got used to the idea of having celebrities in town, they'd close ranks to protect the Sinclairs from scoundrels like this pesky paparazzo.

Rocky and Adam stopped when they saw the people clustered by the gym door. Rocky smiled at Molly. "You're Fergus's friend, right? From the bakery?"

Molly flushed. "Molly Ferris. And these are my friends." She made introductions.

"We met Trent at his store." Adam shook Trent's hand. "Now I feel I could take on the elements if I had to. Not that I want to. I'm more than happy to be cozy inside, what with my thin SoCal blood."

Molly watched Laura glance from Rocky to Adam and back to Rocky, comparing the two men. It was strange how much they appeared alike, yet were so different.

"We're going to be your cooks during the storm." Laura indicated Carol, Molly, and herself. "Any requests?"

"Laura's the one who made those Scottish snowballs Adrian liked so much," Molly added.

Rocky laughed. "He who is stingy with his carbohydrates ate three." He turned to Adam. "Here's a Lou Duckworth shot. Adrian eating a Scottish snowball with the tagline, 'Sad last days of Adrian Sinclair as he eats his way to the grave.'" Disgust lined Rocky's tone.

Adam snorted. "Adrian's smile would make a lie of that line."

A man appeared at the door of the gym. He wasn't as tall as Rocky or Adam, but he was as fit a person as Molly had ever seen. "Hi," he said. "I'm Chet Tudor. I manage the gym and weight area. You're Rocky and Adam, right? I've been waiting for you."

Although Chet didn't sound the least bit upset, Rocky made a little apologetic noise. "And I'm sure you want to get home. Sorry for holding you up." He followed Chet into the room with Adam close behind.

"Not a problem," Chet said. "Let me take you through what's available."

As the three men walked into the exercise area, three things happened at once.

Rocky tripped over the edge of a machine as he cut a corner.

Chet reached out to steady him.

And a gunshot rang out, shattering the silence.

4

There was a split second of stunned silence, then everything broke loose at once.

"Shooter!" Chet yelled. "Everyone down!"

Molly fell to her knees outside the gym's door as Rocky, Adam, and Chet ducked in the gym. Laura dropped too, and Trent put a protective arm around her. Carol and Harvey crouched with their arms about each other.

Molly held her breath. There were no other shots, so presumably the shooter had moved on.

Rocky and Chet straightened, but Adam slid toward the ground in slow motion. One hand went out to stop his fall. The other clutched his chest.

"Adam?" Rocky lunged for his friend and caught him before his head hit the floor. "He's bleeding!" His voice was ragged with shock as he helped Adam lie down.

"Here. Press hard." Chet shoved towels at Rocky, who pushed them against Adam's wound.

"Hang on, Adam. You're going to be fine." Rocky's anguish for his friend was evident.

The noise of the shot brought several other people running from the direction of the den. Fergus was in the lead, with Paula and Trace right behind him. Bobby Elder and the agent, Jonathan Hooper, were last.

Trace saw everyone staring into the gym. "Rocky!" His young face contorted with fear as he forced his way to the door.

Rocky held up a hand. "I'm okay, Trace. I'm okay. It's Adam."

Trace pushed past Laura and Molly and fell to his knees beside his friend. Molly remembered the wink Adam had given Trace and the affection between the two. Poor kid. Seeing his friend hurt must be tearing his heart open, and he'd already been through so much in his young life.

Fergus held his phone up. "I'm calling 911."

Molly straightened, but she didn't know what to do next. There had to be something she could do, should do to help. She just didn't know what it was.

Paula, standing in the doorway, murmured to Jonathan, "It's only Adam. If it had been Rocky—"

Jonathan's expression was knowing. "Catastrophe."

Molly stared at them in disbelief. What was wrong with them? Adam wasn't an "only." No one was.

"But Rocky saving a life? Pure gold." Paula took several pictures of Rocky and Chet working to stop the flow of Adam's blood. "Matt Bryant in the flesh."

"Love it." Jonathan took a few photos of his own. "With the film opening, this couldn't have happened at a better time."

Rocky must have heard their conversation because he rounded on them. "What do you think you're doing?" His rage could have melted the ice cap outside.

Paula's eyes went wide, and she took a step back. Jonathan held his ground, but he swallowed, a kid caught with his hand in the cookie jar.

Rocky pointed at Paula. "If any picture of this or anything else that happens here shows in print or online, I will see that you are fired. Do you understand?"

Paula nodded, her skin a sickly gray.

Rocky then glared at Jonathan. "And you. You will lose Adrian and me as clients, along with as many others as I can talk into leaving with us. Adam is not to be exploited." The blazing anger on Rocky's features morphed into disgust. "And *never* refer to my friend as an 'only.' Understand?" He scowled at Jonathan until the agent dropped his gaze, and then his expression melted into gentle concern as he concentrated on his friend.

Molly felt like cheering. She glanced at Carol and Laura and knew she would have done the same for them. That was what friends did for each other. They spoke up and they protected. Still, impressed as she was, she realized she never wanted to get on Rocky's bad side.

Trace sat quietly on the floor beside Adam, holding his hand and talking to him. Molly was impressed by the boy's calm manner as he spoke. The wounded man didn't respond at first, and Molly feared it was a lot worse than she'd thought. Then Adam managed a wink for the boy. Molly felt the knot of anxiety in her chest loosen.

Fergus gave one of those whistles that silenced any crowd, and everyone shifted their focus to him. "The police are on the way, and the ambulance will be here any minute," he announced. "We'll merely make their job harder if we stay here and get in their way. Let's go to the den so that when they arrive, they have room to work." He began herding everyone back down the hall.

Molly knew what she could do to help. "I'll go wait in the lobby to tell the police and EMTs where to come." She started to walk in that direction.

"That's not safe, Molly." Fergus stopped and frowned. "There's an active shooter somewhere."

"I'll go with her." Laura volunteered, following Molly.

"Me too." Carol hurried to catch up, ignoring Harvey's protests behind her.

Molly expected Fergus to argue, but Jonathan pulled his attention away. She, Laura, and Carol continued to the lobby, where they paused by the front door of Castleglen and stared at each other.

"What just happened?" Laura asked.

Molly's heart was still pounding. "All I know is that it was a single shot, likely a targeted shooting. Whoever it was didn't fire on all of us. He didn't fire on Rocky and Chet at all, even though they were right there."

Carol ran a hand through her hair. "Do you really think Adam was the intended target? I mean, why would anyone shoot him?"

Laura frowned. "We don't know anything about his personal life. For all we know, there's a long line of people who dislike him."

"And one of them is here?" Carol didn't sound convinced.

Molly thought back to her conversation with Trace. "His girlfriend's ex is a problem, and there's a blackmailer Adam reported to the police who's now in deep trouble. They both dislike him."

"But would they be here?" Carol shook her head. "That isn't likely, especially considering the weather."

"Yeah, but the other Californians managed to get here," Laura pointed out. "Maybe someone who dislikes Adam did too."

Molly thought back to when everything happened. "Rocky tripped, remember? Chet reached for him. The shot was fired while all that movement was happening. Maybe whoever it was wanted Rocky, but Adam was hit when Rocky almost fell?"

"That makes more sense to me," Carol said. "Wouldn't the more famous person be the target?"

"Ladies." A familiar resonant voice spoke from behind Molly. She whirled to see Adrian approaching them from the elevators. He reached them as a police car, its lights flashing, pulled under the canopy.

Chief Owen Thomson climbed out and ran into the lobby. He raised an eyebrow in question at Molly.

"Down there." Molly pointed. "In the gym."

As he hurried off, the ambulance pulled in behind his cruiser, followed by another police vehicle.

Adrian's eyes went wide with worry. "What happened?"

"Someone shot Adam," Molly said.

The color drained from Adrian's face. "Rocky? Trace?"

"They're fine, both of them," Laura assured him.

"They were going to the gym," Adrian said. "I didn't want to go. I stayed in my room."

The EMTs rushed in, and Molly waved them toward the gym. They ran in that direction, and Adrian followed. Officers Greer Anderson and Dalziel Murdoch, streaming rain and sleet from their regulation slickers, paused to make sure the Bakehouse Three were all right, then also headed for the gym.

Laura and Carol made as if to walk that way too, but Molly put a hand on their arms. "Do you remember the name that Rocky and Adam mentioned before all this happened? The man Rocky got the restraining order against?"

Laura and Carol glanced at each other. Laura said, "Lou something."

"An animal of some sort," Carol offered. "Oh, I remember. Lou Duckworth."

"Right." Molly got her phone. "How do you think you spell Lou?"

"You try L-o-u, and I'll try L-e-w," Laura said.

"I have it," Molly said after a few moments of screen tapping. She held out her phone so Laura and Carol could see. "He's a paparazzo."

The images showed a slight man with a receding hairline and a camera slung around his neck. The lens seemed bigger than he was. With the odd sense that she knew him from somewhere, Molly. clicked through to his website and found picture after picture of celebrities. For every single shot of someone else, there were five of Rocky.

Laura peered over her shoulder. "I can't imagine what it would be like to have someone stalking me like that, recording everything I did."

"How could you have a private life?" Carol added.

"You move up here." The location made sense to Molly now.

"Do you think this guy followed Rocky?" Laura asked.

Molly thought of the little man who had raced across the bakehouse's parking lot. "I know he did. He's right here in Loch Mallaig. I saw him." She told Laura and Carol about the shadow on the porch and the man in the lot.

Carol frowned. "So he was trying to shoot Rocky and got Adam instead?"

"I suppose," Molly replied. "Though why he'd want to shoot his golden goose with anything but a camera is beyond me."

"Maybe he tried to injure Rocky because of the picture potential?" Laura immediately shook her head at her own suggestion. "That's a pretty big risk. What if he'd killed him by mistake? No more pictures. Not to mention that shooting people lands you in jail."

Molly paced slowly toward the gym and the den beyond it, and her friends followed. "I get that scandalous pictures of Rocky, or Adrian for that matter, would make Duckworth a lot of money, but taking the risk of shooting him? I agree. It doesn't make sense."

"People aren't always rational," Laura said.

They passed the darkened restaurants in silence, lost in their thoughts.

"I've got another question," Molly said as they approached the gym. "Where was the shooter hiding? He couldn't have been in the gym and weight room. Rocky, Adam, or the manager, Chet, would have seen him."

"Is there a locker room beside the gym?" Carol asked. "I bet there is. The pool's down that way too, so a locker room would make sense.

Guests don't want to traipse through the lobby in their swimsuits or workout gear."

As they approached the gym, the EMTs wheeled Adam out on a gurney. He was pale, his breathing shallow, his skin clammy. An IV feed went into one arm, an oxygen cannula lay on his upper lip, and an EMT talked to him in an effort to keep shock at bay. Adam did not respond.

Dear God, Molly prayed, *please let him be okay.* The drive to the more advanced hospital in Marquette would take an hour and a half, longer with the slick roads. A lot could go wrong in that time. *Please take care of him.*

Rocky emerged from the gym, eyes fixed on the gurney. "I'm going with him. Adrian, stay with Trace."

Chief Thomson stepped in front of Rocky and shook his head. "Normally I wouldn't have any trouble with you going, but this weather is too dangerous for a California driver. I don't want to put my people at risk when they have to rescue you because you slid off the road."

Rocky drew himself to his full, very impressive height, ready to fight. Grief, fear, and anger flew over his expression in waves. "I'm going."

Chief Thomson put a gentle hand on his arm. "You can't do anything for your friend. He's in good hands."

"But it's Adam," Rocky said in anguish.

"Don't go, Rocky." Trace grabbed Rocky's other arm. "Please. Don't go."

"Rocky." Adam's whisper somehow cut through all the other noise and voices.

Rocky hurried to his friend's side.

"Don't come." His voice was a thread of sound. "Too dangerous."

"But . . ." Rocky's eyebrows knit in apprehension.

"Adam's right, Rocky," Adrian said. "The chief's right. He'll be well cared for, and we don't want you risking yourself when you can't do anything anyway. Adam knows you care and would go if things were different. But we need you here. Trace needs you here."

Rocky clearly read the fear in his little brother's face and gave in. "Okay."

"Go join the others in the den and give your statements to my officers," the chief said. His tone was kind, but it was an order.

Rocky stood helplessly as Adam continued his journey to the waiting ambulance. When he disappeared from sight, the three Sinclairs started down the hall to the den.

"Send out Fergus MacGregor and Greer Anderson," the chief called after them. He stood in the doorway to the gym, staring at the crime scene as he waited for Fergus and Greer. He ignored Molly, Carol, and Laura, who stood quietly and watched.

Fergus appeared in no time, Greer a few feet behind him. "What can I do for you, Chief?" he asked.

"You've had a shooting in your resort, Fergus," the chief replied. "And you have a famous actor who may well have been the target."

Fergus frowned. "You don't think Adam was the intended victim?"

Thomson remained impassive. "I don't know. Maybe. I need to learn more about him before I can make a judgment. Unfortunately, I don't have the manpower for an exhaustive search, so I advise everyone staying here to stick together. And I'm leaving an officer here as a sort of bodyguard for Rocky Sinclair."

"Not a problem," Fergus agreed. "Who?"

The chief jerked his head in Greer's direction. Greer blinked and took a step back, obviously startled—and likely not very happy.

"She's experienced and capable," the chief told Fergus. "You can trust her to do her job."

"Of course," Fergus said. "I'll see she has all she needs while she's here."

The chief signaled Greer over. She still wore her rain slicker, her countenance crunched into a frown. "You still keep a change of clothes in your vehicle?" he asked her.

"A few, actually," she answered. "You never know what's going to happen."

"You're going to need them," Thomson said. "I want you to stay here and be Rocky Sinclair's bodyguard."

"But, sir—"

He held up a hand to stop her. "I'll see you get overtime, but I'm not sure if I can get them to agree to hardship pay when you get to stay at Castleglen." He smiled at what he obviously considered a joke.

"But what about the storm?" Greer protested. "I can't stay here. I need to be available to help."

"You need to be here. That's what you've been ordered to do."

"Wouldn't Murdoch be better?" she asked. "A guy protecting a guy."

"We're not negotiating, Anderson." The chief fixed his steely gaze on her. "You have an assignment."

Greer took a deep breath and said, "Yes, sir," but her displeasure was obvious.

Molly remembered Greer's disparaging comments when the Sinclairs first came into Bread on Arrival. If the situation hadn't been so serious, the assignment would be funny. Considering the circumstances, perhaps the chief thought the fact that Greer was anything but starstruck would help her keep a clear head.

Rocky came out of the den. "Chief, we need to talk about how to keep me and my family safe."

"Officer Anderson will provide protective service for you," Chief Thomson said. "She will stay by your side as long as you're here."

The only person who appeared more appalled by the situation than Greer was Rocky.

Still, Molly thought with a chill, they were blizzard bound in a vast resort with a would-be murderer who may not have finished the job he set out to do. They were lucky to have any police protection at all.

5

Night seemed to fall earlier than usual, with the rain and sleet still tumbling from the sky and transforming into an ever-thickening ice crust as soon as it hit. After a quick trip to the frosty front lawn, Molly returned to her room with Angus, who had been glad to keep his outdoor visit brief. She had been glad he'd been out of harm's way during the shooting, and although she wished she could keep him close now, she knew he was safer in her room. She bent and patted him. "I know you miss the action, but you'll be warm and safe here."

His tail wagged at her cheerful tone, his eyebrows waggled, and he trotted to a spot in front of the room's built-in gas fireplace, where he sprawled out with a happy sigh.

Molly smiled as she left him, glad she had dinner preparations to take her mind off both the weather and poor Adam. The attack preyed on her nerves as she hurried through the resort's deserted halls, however. She couldn't forget the very real possibility that there was still a shooter at large somewhere in the building. The police had been unable to say for certain whether the gunman had made a getaway or remained on the grounds, a fact that made Molly so uneasy that she practically ran to the kitchen, where she, Laura, and Carol got to work organizing dinner.

Adrian joined them a few minutes later. "Rocky is calling Adam's girlfriend, but I've got idle hands," he reported solemnly. "Can I help?"

Laura blinked, and Molly suppressed a chuckle. What would her former hotshot chef friend say to a big-time Hollywood star used to getting his way and who Laura likely thought would get in her way?

He beamed at them. "If I hadn't fallen into the acting gig, I'd have been a chef. Let me help. It'd make my day. And keep me from worrying about Adam."

Laura shrugged her agreement, and in no time, she and Adrian were at the stove, her grilling chicken breasts, him making his patented barbecue sauce.

"It's literally patented," he explained. "Or is it trademarked? I always get them confused. Anyway, when I can't get movie parts anymore, I'll start a food business. My barbecue sauce will be the first item produced."

He offered Laura a taste, and she hummed in approval. While his sauce simmered, he cut up onions and potatoes, seasoned them, and wrapped them in aluminum foil packets that he put in the oven to brown. Molly was impressed at the practiced ease of his movements.

Carol made a huge salad and a batch of her signature dressing. After one bite, Adrian offered to buy the recipe for his food business. "I'll make it well worth your while," he told her.

Carol grinned. "My retirement is now secure."

Molly organized the serving of the meal with Harvey and Trent's help. They set up two tables in the hall outside the den for a buffet line and two tables inside with seats for fourteen. They grabbed linens, china, and cutlery from Tee for Two.

"Just because we're doing our meals seat-of-the-pants doesn't mean we have to lower Castleglen's standards," she assured Fergus.

"You are an amazing woman." His approval made her smile so broadly that Carol and Laura laughed at her. Trent didn't bother to hide a proud grin.

Laura had Trent and Harvey carry a table from Tee for Two to the den, where she made a coffee bar in one corner. She was checking cream and sugar when Greer walked into the room. Earlier, after interviewing all the guests regarding their whereabouts during the shooting—and apparently coming up without a viable suspect among them—the woman had stomped off, a frustrated cop unhappy over her assignment, her duffel gripped in one hand. She'd been given a private bedroom connected to the Sinclairs' expansive suite, where she'd retreated to change. She returned wearing jeans, a deep green sweater that made her eyes pop, and sleek leather boots. Her blonde hair was combed free and curled down her back. Molly thought she looked great.

Molly was tickled that the room went quiet when Greer entered. Her transformation startled everyone into silence, even Bobby Elder, who saw her in civilian clothes at least once a week at church. The California crowd gaped, especially Rocky. Molly could practically see his mind readjusting to having Greer watch over him. When she came to take a seat beside him at the table—she was, after all, his bodyguard—he stood to hold her chair. She glared at him for the courtesy.

Paula took a seat across the table from Greer. "Did you have to go to school to learn police stuff?" she asked. "I mean, like the men did?"

Greer studied Paula as if trying to discern her motives for asking such a foolish and obvious question. Was Paula being merely curious, or was she trying to make Greer feel uncomfortable? "My undergraduate degree from Michigan State is in criminal justice," Greer finally answered. "Then I went to the police academy, like all the men and women who become police officers."

"Was it hard?" Paula seemed genuinely curious. "I mean, you're gorgeous."

Greer blinked. "It was tough." She stared down beautiful Paula. "My appearance had nothing to do with it."

Paula dropped her gaze and began fiddling with her hair.

Adrian appeared in the doorway. "Dinner is served. Come help yourselves."

Greer stood, obviously relieved that something new had become the focus of attention.

While temperatures outside continued to fall, Molly thought the atmosphere at dinner was warm and convivial—as long as she didn't think about the crime scene down the hall. While they ate, Rocky periodically stepped outside to call the hospital in Marquette for updates on Adam.

"He's arrived at the hospital," he announced initially. "Finally."

"They're prepping him for emergency surgery," Rocky added a short while later, his face grim. "He's lost an awful lot of blood."

"He's out of surgery and in the ICU," came the latest news. "The doctors said they did all they could, but he's in rough shape. The next twenty-four hours will be critical." After the last report Rocky closed his eyes as if in pain. "I don't know what I'll do if he dies. I should have gone with him."

"Don't, Rocky." Adrian patted him on the back.

"You're right." Rocky rubbed his temples. "His girlfriend wants to fly here, but the airports are closed."

"Jill couldn't do anything to help him any more than you could," Adrian said. He gestured at Rocky's mostly untouched plate. "Eat. You have to keep up your strength."

After dinner dishes were cleared, Molly served dessert from a table in the hallway. Offerings consisted of leftover sweets from the display cases at Bread on Arrival, as well as a chocolate cake with caramel frosting that Carol had made for a special order canceled due to the weather.

Bobby smiled as he accepted a second slice of cake from Molly. "I could get used to eating like this."

Fergus, who was standing in line to get his own second slice, asked, "Are you planning on staying at Castleglen tonight, Bobby?"

"Of course not," Bobby said smoothly. "I'll leave as soon as I've finished eating." He gave a laugh. "It's not as if I can show the Sinclairs any property for a few days."

Molly watched Bobby and suspected that in spite of his protests, he wanted to remain at Castleglen so he could continue to talk to Adrian and Rocky about the wonders of life in Loch Mallaig.

Judging by his shrewd expression, Fergus was likely thinking the same thing as Molly. He met her eyes and gave a little shrug as his innate hospitality overpowered the likelihood that he was being taken advantage of. "You can't leave in this weather, Bobby. We've got plenty of rooms."

"That would be swell, Fergus. I don't relish the thought of driving home on those roads." Bobby beamed. "I'll pay, of course."

"I'm happy to have you on one condition," Fergus said sternly. "You are not to bother the Sinclairs. No selling. No pictures. No nothing."

Molly bit back a smile. Fergus could be quite intimidating when he put his mind to it.

Bobby swallowed hard and disappeared into the den as Paula emerged.

The young woman glanced around with a frown, then zeroed in on Molly. "Is there peppermint tea anywhere?"

Molly knew she'd set out several kinds of tea, including peppermint. Perhaps the weather had made mint sound good to several people. "Sure. Let me get some more."

She dashed down the hall to Tee for Two and grabbed several bags of peppermint. As she hurried back past the gym, she heard water running and stopped to investigate. She stepped into the room and hit the light switch. Chief Thomson had let Chet clean up the blood pooling on the wooden floor before the floor warped, causing expensive damage. Had Chet accidentally left a faucet running that had overflowed?

No, it was much worse than that.

What in the world? Molly slapped a hand over her mouth as she saw a large crack near the bottom of one of the floor-to-ceiling windows that looked out over the golf course. Water was gushing into the room through the starburst at the base of the crack, flooding the floor. The potential for damage was much greater than that from the blood.

She bolted for the den and burst through the door. "Fergus, the gym is flooding!"

Fergus and everyone else in the den followed her back to the gym at a run, desserts and peppermint tea forgotten.

Fergus crossed the room, his shoes disturbing the standing water and sending drops this way and that. He crouched to examine the window and the water flooding the wooden gym floor, then returned to the group crowded around the doorway.

"It's the rain sliding off the snow and ice," Fergus reported. "The snowpack near the building is lower because of the heat from the building, and there's a swathe of ground against the building that is usually clear. Normally, the rain that runs off the snow travels into the drains there, but the ice buildup is keeping the rain from following its usual course, and the break in the window gives the water somewhere to go. Gravity was all that was needed to create this mess."

"I'll get my coat," Harvey said.

"Mine's in my office," Fergus replied. "I'll meet you in the lobby."

"Right behind you," Trent offered.

"Coat?" Bobby's expression was horrified as he peered at the world outside the windows.

"We have to go out and dig a trench to direct the water away from the building," Fergus explained.

"Outside?" Jonathan, the agent, made a choking sound. "In this?"

"Yes, outside in this," Fergus said. "Who wants to help Harvey, Trent, and me?"

Rocky and Chet signaled their willingness.

Trace made an unhappy face, but nodded.

"I'll help too," Adrian said. "I'm not an old man yet."

"I'll meet you all at the door," Greer said, then started for the suite and her outdoor gear.

Rocky put out a hand to stop her. "Not you."

Greer stiffened. "Why not? I have to be where you are."

"There are more than enough men to take care of the situation."

"Men?" Greer repeated sharply. Clearly he'd hit a nerve. "I am not some poor little woman to be protected from discomfort and cold. I can more than hold my own out there."

"I'm sure you can." Rocky leaned toward her, hands on his hips, anger making his shoulders stiff. "I'm not trying to 'protect' you." She gave a disbelieving snort, and he continued, "I'm trying to be nice."

Fergus waved his hands at them. "And while you two yell at each other, water's pouring into my gym. I call the shots here. Rocky, you come with me. Greer, you stay here."

Her head shot up, outrage plain on her features.

"Don't give me that look. You're in charge of saving my floor." With that, Fergus stalked from the room. "And figure out what to do about that window," he called back over his shoulder.

Rocky followed Fergus, satisfied. Greer frowned, apparently uncertain whether she'd won or lost.

"The supply room's there." Chet pointed as he headed for his office, where he likely kept his coat. "Lots of towels and buckets."

Molly noted that Bobby and Jonathan disappeared after Fergus and the others. She imagined them slipping away to the comfort of their rooms and staying there. Paula had left as soon as she saw the water on the floor, likely in the interest of preserving the turquoise boots she still wore.

Under Greer's direction, each of the four remaining women grabbed several towels and a bucket. They began mopping, wringing the frigid water into the buckets, and mopping again. When the buckets filled, they lugged them into the locker room and poured the water down the shower drain. Molly had rarely done a more frustrating job. The water gushed in faster than they could mop it up.

"What if you hadn't found this when you did?" Carol pushed her hair off her forehead before mopping again. "I can't imagine the damage."

Even with the outdoor lights on, the men were shadows through the downpour, chopping at the ice with axes and shovels to break through to the snow, digging deeper and deeper as they moved away from the building, hoping to guide the water away. Molly was struck by what an engineering feat they were working on, all angles and trajectory. As their trench grew, the flow slowed. After several minutes, it became a mere trickle.

Molly straightened her aching back and jumped when she saw Fergus and Rocky outside the window. Their heads bent, they walked back and forth in the narrow swathe near the foundation that remained uncovered by snow. Fergus stopped and reached down. When he stood, he had a large plastic bag in his hand. His expression was serious.

Greer stood beside Molly, watching. "That must have clogged the drain. If someone did it intentionally, that makes it deliberate destruction."

Molly crossed her arms over her chest. "Considering how pristine the grounds are, I'm afraid it's likely that someone did leave it there."

Laura flexed her hands. "My hands have never been so cold."

"My feet are freezing too." Carol gestured to her wet clogs.

"Let's get this window patched so we can go warm up," Greer said. "We need duct tape."

A cold, wet Chet appeared, shivering as he pulled off his drenched coat. "I've got some." He went into his office, leaving a trail of water behind him, and reappeared with two rolls of tape in his hands and a gym bag slung over his shoulder. He tossed one roll of tape to Greer and one to Molly, then held up his duffel. "Fergus just gave me a room. I'm going there to have a hot shower and change before I catch pneumonia."

Carol managed to find a dry towel and mopped up behind Chet. Then the women stood back and examined the window and its fissure, noting the circle of crazed glass above floor level from which the crack radiated.

"Someone used something heavy to break the window." Molly swallowed hard. "Someone deliberately made this trouble."

Greer pulled her phone from her pocket and took several pictures. "A sledgehammer?" She glanced over her shoulder at the weights stacked neatly in the corner of the weight room. "Or a dumbbell. Whatever it was, there's no doubt. This room is a crime scene." Her face was grim. "Again."

6

Molly found it hard to believe, but the whole window incident had taken only thirty minutes from discovery to duct tape. It was now nine o'clock, six o'clock for the California people. Eventually everyone changed into dry clothing and settled back in the den, where they could stay warm by the roaring fire. Molly brought Angus along, so their progress down the hallway was slow as he sniffed the baseboards.

Fergus was speaking with Greer outside the door to the den. "It's sabotage," he said, his voice clipped. "But I have no idea why."

"I've reported it to the chief and sent him my photos," Greer said. "I need to talk to everyone here and learn what they saw, if anything."

"Please do," Fergus agreed. "Find out everything you can."

"Of course, but please remember that my primary job here is to keep an eye on Rocky Sinclair."

"I know, and I respect that. But someone inside my building is intent on harm. We need to find him before he tries something else."

"Is it the same person who shot Adam?" Molly asked as she and Angus reached Fergus and Greer.

"That's the question we have to answer," Fergus said gravely.

"How did this person get into the building, Fergus?" Greer asked. "What other doors are there someone could enter?"

"All doors were locked shortly after the ambulance left," he answered. "There's a buzzer at the front that will let me know if anyone comes during the night, but otherwise we're locked in and anyone else is locked out. The alarm system will let us know if there's a breach."

Greer approved the safety measures, and they all went into the den to join the others. While Angus went to greet Carol and Laura, the officer began circulating, asking each person what they'd seen. The answer was always the same if the shaking heads were any indication. No one had noticed anything.

"I don't know what kind of a place this is," Jonathan blustered loudly after his brief conversation with Greer. "A good friend shot. A malicious act against our host. A nightmare weather system. I have never felt so unsafe in my life."

Molly mentally rolled her eyes at the dramatics. Everyone else was managing the same scenario with grace.

Greer turned back to him with interest. "Does someone have a motive to harm you, Mr. Hooper? Is that why you feel threatened?"

Jonathan's chest puffed in outrage. "A motive to harm me? How can you ask such a thing?"

Greer stood her ground. "How can I not?"

"Impertinent, disrespectful locals," Jonathan snapped at Rocky, who stood off to one side. "Another of many reasons for you to reconsider moving here."

Rocky took a sip from his steaming cup of coffee. "Not your call to make, Jonathan, as I've said repeatedly. By the way, your 'good friend'—whom you haven't once asked about—is still fighting for his life." Rocky's voice caught. "It will be a while before they know if he'll survive."

Jonathan didn't appear the least embarrassed by Rocky calling him out on his fabricated concern for Adam.

Greer took over the conversation. "Did you see anyone unexpected when you were moving about the building, Mr. Hooper?" When he shook his head, she added, "Not even when you were on your own while the men were outside and we were cleaning up?"

Jonathan raised an eyebrow. "If I saw anything, I would have said so."

The icy disdain in his voice would have made anyone else step back, but Greer returned it with a cool smile of her own. "Thank you. If you think of anything, please let me know."

Molly watched Jonathan stalk to the coffee bar, where he topped off his cup before moving to the cushiest seat by the fire. He might be a talented agent—certainly Rocky and Adrian had done very well under his care—but he was not a nice man. His success had made him condescending and entitled.

Greer spoke with Bobby, then Paula, and Molly could no longer hear what was being said. She moved to the coffee bar to check how supplies were holding up.

Trace came up behind her, a cup of hot chocolate in his hand. "What if more water gets in?" he asked fretfully. "What if all that duct tape on the window doesn't hold and the gym floods again? What if the trench fills in and we have to go out again? What if someone else gets shot? What if Adam—"

Molly placed her hand over one of his as he clutched his mug. "How's your hot cocoa?"

He blinked as his what-ifs were interrupted. "Um, delicious."

"Laura has a special recipe, with a drop of vanilla and a dash of cinnamon."

"Okay." Trace was still a bit wide-eyed, but his anxiety was clearly dissipating.

Molly smiled. "Those cinnamon-sugar doughnuts on the dessert table go especially well with it. They really bring out the cinnamon flavor."

Trace's eyes lit at the sight of the table against the back wall laden with the remains of dessert and new additions like the doughnuts. Molly could see his priorities realign.

"Help yourself," she told him. "And don't worry about the window. It's secure. Fergus and Chet nailed a piece of plywood over the glass for extra support. They also put some electric space heaters in the area to help dry everything. The drain outside has been cleared, so the backup won't happen again. You won't have to go out. As to the rest, Adam is strong, so if anyone can survive being shot, it's him. And you don't have to worry about your brother. Greer is one of our top officers. No one could keep him safer than she will."

"You're sure?"

"Positive." Molly said, patting his shoulder. Trace was so tall it was easy to forget he was still very young.

"This whole thing is wild." He shook his head. "If I was home, I would be sitting by the pool with a frosty drink in my hand."

Rocky walked up, Greer beside him, and gave Trace a light punch on the arm. "At home, you'd be in your room doing homework right about now. Enjoy the break."

"Sometimes homework is preferable," Trace mumbled.

Fergus leaned in. "But think of the stories you can tell your friends back home. Have any of them had the privilege of saving a historic resort from disaster? Would any of them have been brave enough to work through the cold and sleet? You stepped up when you were needed in spite of the danger."

"It's exactly the kind of thing a Marine would do, because it was necessary and right rather than easy or glamorous," Molly added.

Trace became thoughtful, and Molly could see him reframing his role in the trench digging. She'd love to hear the version he would finally tell his friends. The boy's pensive expression became eager, and Molly suspected his quick change of direction meant they should beware of his next idea.

"Hey, Mr. MacGregor," he said. "When we were out there, I saw you have a hot tub. Is it still working?"

Fergus shrugged. "It is, but it's awfully nasty weather for sitting in a hot tub."

Rocky eyed his brother. "Why don't you use the indoor pool?"

"I can use an indoor pool any place," Trace said. "I can't sit in a hot tub in a winter storm anywhere but here."

Rocky considered his brother. "I thought you didn't want to go out in this weather again."

"This is different. Maybe I'll try it tomorrow." With an anticipatory smile, Trace wandered off to the dessert table, where Molly saw him pick up two cinnamon-sugar donuts.

Rocky watched him with an indulgent smile, Greer with interest.

Fergus took Molly's hand. "Sit with me a few minutes?" he asked, and she instantly agreed.

He led her to one of the leather love seats, where they made themselves comfortable. Angus broke away from sitting on Harvey's foot to jump into her lap. She studied Fergus's weary face as he leaned back in his seat. An attempted murder and industrial sabotage in one evening tended to take it out of a person.

"Are you okay?" she asked quietly.

"I think so." He reached over and scratched the top of Angus's head, and the little dog climbed from Molly's lap to his.

"Smart boy," Fergus told him as he settled against him. "We guys have to stick together."

"Traitor." Molly chucked Angus under the chin, and he kissed her on the nose.

Paula appeared at Molly's side. "Did you ever get that peppermint tea I asked for? I could sure use some to soothe my nerves."

Molly got to her feet. "Sorry. I got sidetracked by the mini-flood." She led the way to the coffee bar, Paula in her turquoise boots right behind her. She glanced back at Fergus and saw Adrian had settled in her vacated seat. Fergus grinned at her over Adrian's head, winked, and returned his attention to his friend.

Molly flipped open the tea chest, and there sat half a dozen packets of peppermint tea right where she had put them before dinner, between the orange spice and the chamomile. As she showed these bags to Paula, she wondered what she had done with the packets she had collected from Tee for Two before the flood. She also wondered why she hadn't thought to check the tea chest before she ran to the kitchen.

Thank goodness she hadn't. If she had, she never would have walked past the gym.

Paula frowned. "That's peppermint? You're sure?"

Molly bit her tongue to keep from reading out loud the word *peppermint* printed across the foil packets in large letters.

Paula reached for one. "It's not what I'm used to."

Molly poured her a mug of hot water. "I'm sure it will taste fine."

Paula suspiciously tore open a packet and lowered the bag into the steaming water. She added a packet of artificial sweetener.

Paula struck Molly as the odd man out in the California gang. Jonathan was professionally involved with both Rocky and Adrian. Adam was professionally and personally attached to Rocky. Trace was anchored by his brother and uncle, who in turn anchored each other. No one seemed to be connected with Paula.

"Why did you come to Loch Mallaig, Paula?" Molly asked.

"Work." Paula took a tentative sip of her tea.

"For the studio?"

"Sol Rosenberg sent me when he heard Jonathan and Adam were flying up." She deepened her voice in imitation of a man. "'If they're going, so are you, Prentiss.'"

"Who's Sol Rosenberg?"

"My boss. He's the guy in charge of the promotion and publicity for *No Death Too Small*."

Paula gazed expectantly at Molly, who felt compelled to shake her head. The name meant nothing to her.

The younger woman groaned. "The latest Matt Bryant film. See? You didn't know its name. If I'd done my job right, you'd know." Her knuckles were white with the force of her grip on her mug. Distress marred her pretty features. "I'm going to lose my job. I know it."

"Because I don't know the name of the movie?"

"Because I haven't done my job if you don't know."

"Isn't it enough that I know there's a new Matt Bryant movie?"

"Sol says no. He says you won't go see it if you don't know its name."

"Interesting theory."

"Do you plan to go see it?" Anxiety saturated Paula's voice.

"Maybe." Molly felt she was letting Paula down with her answer and tried to explain. "Loch Mallaig doesn't have a theater. Up here, going to the movies is a planned event. You have to drive a distance, and in winter, you just might choose not to. But don't action movies usually open in the summer? Isn't that when previous Matt Bryant movies released?"

"Usually, but the studio bigwigs decided we needed to capitalize on the coming holiday season. Bring Matt out in a blaze of glory over Thanksgiving weekend, when he could win the screen. Opening weekend numbers are so critical."

"So how did *No Death Too Small* do?"

"It won the weekend."

"Then what's the problem?"

"Sol's boss wants more."

"And Sol dumped it all on you."

"That's right," Paula said miserably. "I need Rocky to do more TV and media, more interviews. Instead, he's hiding out here at some nowhere dot on the map."

Molly remembered Greer's comments in the afternoon. "I heard he was photographed at the premiere and has made lots of other appearances."

"He was very cooperative. He did everything Sol and I asked of him."

"Then what's the matter?"

"He went on vacation."

Molly watched Rocky talking with Adrian and Fergus, his protection stationed at his side. "And Sol wants more," she guessed.

"A lot more, and it's my job to get it," Paula said gloomily.

"Well, you're certainly not going to get anything for the next two or three days," Molly said regretfully.

Paula's phone dinged, and she made a face. "That'll be Sol wanting to know what I've convinced Rocky to do." She pulled it out, tapped the screen, and gasped. Her anxiety dissolved into delighted disbelief. She held out her phone for Molly.

A photo of a laughing Rocky standing beside a beautiful, smiling blonde in a deep green sweater and jeans appeared on a major entertainment site with the caption, *Who is Rocky Sinclair's new girlfriend?* Molly groaned as she recognized the woman.

Greer was going to have a conniption.

Even as Molly watched the little screen, comments appeared beneath the picture.

Yowzah! Beautiful! Lucky Rocky.

You're kidding. Rocky's dating her?

I thought Rocky loved Penny Patterson. Unfaithful rat.

Saw No Death Too Small. *Loved it!*

No Death Too Small *was pure drivel. Save your money.*

Rocky, she's a keeper!

Why do celebrities always go for the blondes? What's wrong with us brunettes?

On and on the comments came, and Paula couldn't stop smiling.

"Did you take that picture?" Molly demanded, Rocky's earlier admonition in her mind.

Paula's grin disappeared and she held up a hand. "I didn't. I swear. But I can practically hear Sol's jaw crack from smiling at this." Her eyes lit up again as she read the hundreds of comments.

"No such thing as bad publicity and all that."

Molly considered the picture again. It had been taken in the hall at dinnertime. Everyone had been milling around and moving through the buffet line. She, Laura, and Carol had been back and forth to the kitchen, making sure there was plenty to go around.

Molly glanced around the den, examining the people. Paula said she hadn't taken the shot. Jonathan then? She didn't think so. The threat of losing Rocky and Adrian would keep his phone in his pocket.

It could have been Bobby Elder, but would he risk losing his lucrative land sale by selling a photo? Besides, he had a crush on Greer. He wouldn't want a picture of her smiling at another man out there for the world to see.

Maybe Chet? The gym manager, in his black T-shirt and rippling muscles, was talking with Bobby about something that made them both unhappy, but she wasn't sure what.

Molly shrugged. She couldn't imagine anyone in the room either taking the photo or knowing what to do with it if they had—except Paula.

"I didn't take it," Paula repeated as Molly's speculative gaze fixed on her again. She blew on her tea. "But I love it."

From the corner of her eye, Molly saw Trace check his phone. His eyes went wide with surprise, and he headed for his brother. When he held out the phone to Rocky, the actor's eyes narrowed, and he scanned the room.

"What is it?" Greer asked Trace. He held out the phone to her, and her expression became horrified. "Are you kidding me?"

"It's a great picture of you, Rocky," Paula said, approaching the group with Molly right behind her. "Not a bad one of you either, Greer."

Greer, a cop to her toes, scowled. "It makes me look like a groupie."

Paula shrugged. "The comments are mostly in your favor so far. There are a few trolls saying nasty things, but most think Rocky has good taste."

"You're famous now," Trace told her, like this was a good thing.

Greer's cheeks flushed. "I don't want to be famous."

Trace shrugged. "Too late."

"Rocky." Greer grabbed his arm. "Do something. Get rid of it. I'm a professional, and I can't have my face splashed all over like some—" She stalled, probably searching for a word that wouldn't insult the Hollywood people all around her. Instead, she groaned. "Come on, I'm a cop."

"Wouldn't that piece of trivia get a great reaction?" Paula all but rubbed her hands together. "Matt Bryant, savior of the world, is dating a cop who saves the world every day."

"He's not dating me." Greer was getting more frustrated by the minute. "I'm his bodyguard. And I don't save the world any more than he does."

"A bodyguard romance." Paula had stars in her eyes. "How much more cinematic can you get? We have to come up with some sort of meet-cute story. We can't tell the truth—that you met at Adam's shooting. It's too negative. Besides, it'd take the attention off Rocky and put it on Adam, which we do not want."

"*We* don't want anything." Greer vibrated with anger. "Stop it."

Paula didn't seem to hear. "Too bad Rocky wasn't the one shot. Then we could say he was injured protecting his bodyguard. Or maybe she saved his life, and as she's caring for him, he's falling for her." Paula all but danced in place at her wonderful ideas.

"Really, Paula?" Molly couldn't believe what she was hearing.

"You can't say I'm a cop." Greer grabbed Paula's arm. "Frankly, you can't identify me at all. I can't have my name dragged through the gossip sites. I have my professional reputation to consider."

Rocky waved a hand as if erasing the online picture and all the comments. "Forget about it, Greer. It'll be gone by tomorrow. Stuff like this is just life for someone like me. You deal by ignoring."

Greer glared at him. "Well it's not 'just life' for someone like me."

"Fair enough," Rocky replied. "Paula, you will not mention Greer in any way. Do you understand me?" He folded his arms, a powerful man waiting for the only acceptable answer.

Color stained Paula's cheeks, but she finally squeaked out an, "Okay."

He cocked his head. "What did you say? I didn't hear you."

She shifted from foot to foot under his scrutiny. "I will not mention Greer." It was little more than a whisper.

"Good girl," Rocky said with approval.

Greer took a deep, calming breath. "Thank you." Molly wasn't sure if she was thanking Rocky for taking her side or Paula for agreeing.

Rocky grabbed Trace's phone, studied the image, then offered the phone to Adrian, who had wandered over to see what all the fuss was about.

"Are you thinking Lou Duckworth?" Adrian asked his nephew, frowning at the phone screen.

"Who's Lou Duckworth?" Bobby was poring over the photo on his own phone. "You look great, Greer." He gave her a toothy smile that she ignored.

"Duckworth's a photographer. A paparazzo." Rocky's voice dripped with scorn.

"He specializes in Rocky," Adrian said. "Stalks him. Follows him everywhere. While the new movie was being shot, Duckworth flew to location and trailed him. At home, he tracks him around town, chases him in the car, barges into restaurants where he's eating."

"He followed me to school once, trying to get pictures of me," Trace said. "Like anybody cares about me."

Rocky reached over and put an arm around Trace's shoulders. "I care about you, kid."

Trace appeared both embarrassed and delighted. "Yeah, yeah."

"He harasses Rocky to the point of danger," Adrian said, "so we got a civil harassment restraining order against him."

"A good idea," Greer said.

"He was at Bread on Arrival earlier." Molly again pictured the little man scurrying to his car, surprised she hadn't thought of him earlier when they'd first seen this photo. She must have been too distracted by everything else happening at the resort. "When you were all there. I saw him run across the parking lot and follow everyone when you left to go to Trent's outfitters."

Everyone shifted their gazes to stare at her.

"You're sure?" Rocky shook his head. "Though why I'm surprised, I don't know." He flicked a hand at the picture. "He's obviously here now."

Greer became all business. "Do you have an order of protection in Michigan? Has he bothered you in any way since you've been here?"

Rocky shook his head. "I never thought he'd follow me here, so I didn't do anything. And no, I haven't seen him."

"Would he have shot Adam, thinking he was you?" Greer asked.

Rocky shook his head. "Why would he shoot me? I make him money. He's a weasel, but he's not someone who shoots people with anything but a camera."

"So maybe the shooter wasn't aiming at you after all," Greer mused aloud. "Maybe Adam really was the target."

"Adam?" Rocky appeared flabbergasted at the thought. "But why?"

"Jill's ex?" Adrian suggested. "Adam's own blackmailer?"

"Hey!" Trace ran to the windows lining the outside wall and pressed himself against the glass. "It's snowing!"

Molly got a kick out of the excitement in the voice of a kid who rarely saw snow, especially coming down as heavily as it was now.

Greer remained focused. "Come on, Rocky, Adrian. Talk to me about Adam." The three of them wandered to a grouping of chairs and became absorbed in evaluating all the reasons Adam could have been targeted.

Molly saw that Laura had been listening intently, and she walked the few feet to join her by the fire. "We've got two different shooters," Molly said.

"One shoots pictures. The other shoots guns," Laura answered glumly.

"And they're both hiding inside Castleglen." Molly shivered. "It's enough to give me the creeps, especially since we can't do anything about it. Let's talk about breakfast. We can control that."

They waved Carol over, and after a few minutes' conversation, Laura clapped her hands to get everyone's attention. "Tomorrow morning, we will be serving scrambled eggs and bacon with toast or pastries as well as all the juice, coffee, and tea you want. We're serving between eight and nine. If you have a problem with this menu for health reasons, let one of us know."

Everybody murmured assent and went back to whatever they'd been doing—relaxing in front of the fire, talking quietly, setting up a jigsaw puzzle. Jonathan pulled out his laptop and began typing. Bobby made believe he wasn't watching Greer. Trace continued to study the snow. As Molly glanced at the boy, he stiffened and moved to the corner of the room at the edge of the window. He squinted intently into the storm.

Paula swanned over to Molly and Laura. "Can I make a request about breakfast?" She brushed her fingers through a section of her long hair that had fallen forward over her shoulder. "If I *have* to eat eggs, I'd prefer egg whites."

"Not a problem," Laura said. "We could also probably find cereal and yogurt somewhere in the kitchen if you'd prefer."

"I usually drink a green smoothie, but yogurt with fresh fruit would be all right." Paula tossed her hair back over her shoulder with the air of one making gracious concessions. "Mango, kiwi, fresh pineapple, cantaloupe, honeydew, and blackberries. I love blackberries."

Molly smiled at Paula's cluelessness. "Sounds good, but this is the Upper Peninsula in the middle of a major storm. We've got limitations. You might have to settle for apples, oranges, and bananas with a few grapes thrown in."

Paula's wrinkle-free brow furrowed. "Oh."

"Adaptability is the name of the game for the next few days, Paula." Molly patted the young woman's arm. "I know you're up for the challenge." *You have to be, or you won't eat.*

Molly wasn't sure who jumped higher—her or Paula—when the security alarm shattered the cozy atmosphere in the den.

8

As the alarm blared, Molly immediately looked to Fergus as the logical person to know what was going on. So did everyone else.

But then Molly discovered Trace was no longer in the room. The last time she'd seen him, he'd been studying the snowfall. Now he wasn't here.

Rocky noticed his brother's absence as well. "Where's Trace?"

"The alarm app says it's a door down the hall," Fergus reported.

Greer raced from the room, Fergus and Rocky on her heels and almost everyone else trailing, even Angus. Jonathan Hooper, however, settled deeper in the comfy chair in front of the fire. When Molly glanced at him, he shrugged.

"I can't do anything about it, so why get up?" he said.

"What if it's a fire?" she asked.

He shrugged again. "I'll smell smoke."

Shaking her head at the thoroughly disagreeable man, Molly continued to the hall, where she found a scowling Greer, a shocked Fergus, a defiant Trace, and a skinny, bedraggled, quivering dog.

Trace, his hair and shoulders dusted with snowflakes, the bottoms of his pants and shoes wet, held the trembling dog in his arms. Snow slid from the animal to the floor in melting plops, one or two hitting Angus as he pranced around Trace's ankles for an introduction to the new friend. Trace clearly expected a reprimand or an argument, but his expression was rebellious.

"You opened the door for the dog?" Fergus's tone wasn't angry, merely curious.

"Yeah." The set of his jaw told Molly that Trace was entirely unapologetic for the chaos he'd caused.

Fergus made certain the door was firmly closed and pushed some commands on his phone. The alarm went blessedly silent, and all Molly could hear were the soothing sounds Trace made to the dog and Angus's impatient panting.

"Angus, come," Molly commanded, and her dog reluctantly abandoned Trace and came to her side.

When Trace saw that everyone was staring at him, he cleared his throat and hugged the dog closer. "He was out there in the cold, in the corner where the building sends out a wing. I could barely make him out. He was trying to find a spot out of the wind, I think."

"I'm glad you wanted to help him," Rocky said gently, "but you should have said something. Fergus could have stilled the alarm before it went off and scared us all."

"I thought the shooter was trying to break back in." Paula wrapped her arms protectively about herself.

"Me too. Or maybe get out." Bobby seemed relieved that he wasn't the only one who'd thought that.

Greer rolled her eyes at both of them, and poor smitten Bobby blushed, likely regretting that he'd admitted his fear. Molly felt like taking Bobby aside and explaining that he was too sensitive—and too much a civilian—for Greer.

Trace turned defensive. "Yeah, well, I forgot about the alarm. All I was thinking was the dog was going to freeze to death, and I had to get to him before he ran off or something."

The scruffy brown mutt had floppy ears and a crooked white blaze on his muzzle. He was some kind of a mix, like no breed Molly had ever seen.

"I've still got a few dry towels in the gym, Trace," Chet said. "I'll get them, and you can dry him off."

Relief flowed from Trace, and Molly could tell he hadn't thought beyond getting the animal out of the weather. "Does he have a collar?" she asked. "Is there an owner we should notify that we have him and he's safe?"

Trace ran his hand around the dog's neck. "No collar."

"Where do you plan to keep him?" Fergus asked, and Molly suppressed a grin. Despite the general no-pets rule at Castleglen—Angus, of course, got special dispensation—Fergus's gracious hospitality extended to animals in the midst of a snowstorm.

"In my room." Trace's voice was hesitant at first. Then he repeated the words as if ready to do battle over them. "In my room."

Fergus didn't contradict the boy. "May I suggest the bathroom? The tile is a bit more dog friendly than the rugs."

"He's a good dog," Trace asserted. "He won't hurt your rugs."

If Molly were a betting woman, she'd put money on the dog spending this and every other night on Trace's bed for years to come .

Chet appeared with a stack of towels. Trace lowered the dog to the ground and took them. He wrapped one around the still quaking animal and began to move it awkwardly along the too-thin body.

"May I help?" Molly knelt beside them and gently rubbed the dog with the towel.

Angus nosed his way forward to greet the frightened pup.

"Whoa, check out the size of these feet." Molly held up one of the puppy's huge paws. "He's still a baby, Trace, and he's going to be a big dog."

"Really?" Trace sat on the floor and ran his hand over the dog's head. The animal gazed at him with canine adoration. "Cool. The last thing I want is one of those little yappy things girls carry around in their purses."

"You're planning to keep him, even after the storm's over?" Rocky eyed his little brother with interest.

Trace's expression became fierce. "He's mine, Rocky." He wrapped a protective arm around the dog. "I found him. I saved him. He's mine."

"Uh-huh," Rocky said as he and Adrian exchanged a glance Molly couldn't quite interpret. "We'll see how you do over the next few days."

When the dog was as dry as he was going to get with a towel, Molly rose. "His stomach is growling. Who knows when he last ate?" She raised an eyebrow at Angus. "Willing to share some of your food?"

He gave a short bark, clearly a yes. Molly grinned. Smart as her Scottie was, it was most likely the word *food* that got the response.

"Take him into the den, Trace, and sit with him by the fire," Molly said. "You can wrap him in another towel. Angus and I will go get some food for him."

"I'll get him a bowl of water." Carol started for the kitchen.

Trace climbed to his feet and picked up the dog, who burrowed into him. "Don't be afraid," he murmured. "I've got you. You're safe."

This time, the expression Rocky and Adrian exchanged was definitely one of satisfaction.

Molly and Angus made a quick trip to their room and returned to the den with half a bag of kibble. Trace sat in one of the big leather chairs, his dog held close. Jonathan sat in the chair next to him, face averted from the boy and the dog. Molly had to acknowledge both boy and puppy smelled like wet dogs, but Jonathan's dour expression seemed a bit overdramatic—especially when he could easily move to another spot.

The others returned to whatever they'd been doing before the alarm sounded. Apart from Jonathan, Molly thought them a nice group of people.

Carol had brought along a bowl for food when she got the dog's water. Molly poured some kibble and set the dish on the floor. The dog sat up straight, quivering not with cold but excitement.

Rocky smiled at his brother. "You've got to let him go for a minute, kid. He's obviously hungry."

Trace reluctantly opened his arms, and the dog jumped to the floor. He checked right and left as if for possible trouble before he rushed the dish. He inhaled the food, then slurped half the bowl of water. Angus stayed by Molly, watching with interest.

When Trace once more held the bedraggled dog close, Fergus walked to a bookshelf and pulled out a hardback book. He held it out to Adrian.

Adrian took it, read the title and began to laugh. "*The Collected Works of Robert Service*. Oh, the memories."

Fergus grinned at Molly. "When we were kids at camp, our counselors would take us into the woods for a campfire and s'mores, and they'd read to us. Ghost stories, adventures, and some of the poems of Robert Service. When we got old enough to be counselors, we read the same things to our campers."

"'The Cremation of Sam Magee.'" Adrian struck a pose and began reciting.

> *There are strange things done in the midnight sun; By the men who moil for gold; The Arctic trails have their secret tales; That would make your blood run cold; The northern lights have seen queer sights; But the queerest they ever did see; Was the night on the marge of Lake LaBarge; I cremated Sam Magee.*

The words rolled off in his trained voice, and Molly could imagine a circle of boys glued to the story of poor warm-blooded Tennessean Sam Magee frozen in the cold Yukon. Everyone in the den stilled and listened.

"My favorite was always 'The Bread-Knife Ballad,'" Fergus said. "So lovely and gory for a boy."

Adrian leafed through the book until he found the poem. He began to read.

> *A little child was sitting upon her mother's knee; And down her cheeks the bitter tears did flow. And as I sadly listened I heard this tender plea; 'Twas uttered in a voice so soft and low. 'Please, Mother, don't stab Father with the bread-knife, Remember 'twas a gift when you were wed. But if you must stab Father with the bread-knife, Please Mother use another for the bread.*

Molly was in the process of taking a drink of coffee as Adrian read the last line. The inhale at the beginning of her laugh made her sputter and have a minor coughing fit. Fergus patted her gently on the back.

"Makes sense to me," Greer said. "Not only is it sanitary to use another knife, but it also prevents contaminating the evidence at the crime scene."

And with no warning, the lights went out.

9

Molly automatically jumped as the room went dark, though the loss of electricity wasn't a particular shock. In a storm this severe, she'd have been surprised if it hadn't gone out. Still, knowing it might happen and having it actually happen were two separate things, and there had already been several unsettling occurrences this evening. Her heart pounded in alarm.

"What's going on here?" Jonathan's sharp voice cut the air, disbelief and disdain evident in his tone. "We're going to be in the dark for the rest of our time here?"

The room wasn't really dark. The fire continued to give off its golden glow, and the emergency light by the door flamed red.

Fergus stood still, head cocked to one side. When nothing happened, he closed his eyes in clear disappointment. The generators weren't kicking on. He went to a closet along one wall and pulled out a very impressive flashlight. "Excuse me." He left the room.

Jonathan continued sputtering in agitation. "This is outrageous."

"Give it a minute, Jonathan." Adrian spoke to his agent as if weary of the man's attitude. "Give Fergus a chance to fix things."

"What's to fix? We've lost power." Jonathan punched the arm of his chair. "What kind of a second-rate place is this?"

No one answered. People shifted awkwardly, undoubtedly thinking much the same as Jonathan but too polite to say anything.

After a few minutes of more complaints from Jonathan, the lights blinked once, then twice, and finally stayed steady. A motor purred somewhere deep in the resort. Everyone breathed a sigh of relief.

Fergus returned and smiled at his guests. "Sorry about the temporary inconvenience. Don't worry. Lights will stay on, and the heat too."

"Whew." Paula sagged with relief. "You had me scared for a second there."

"Will this happen again?" Jonathan asked, all pompous indignation.

"This wing will be fine," Fergus said.

"Only this wing?" Jonathan scowled, appalled. "Our rooms aren't in this wing."

"No," Fergus said, "but we will take good care of you. Don't worry."

Jonathan was too keyed up to listen. "You live with the threat of weather like this every winter, and you don't have a generator capable of providing power to the whole place? What happens if you have a full house and something like this happens?" Jonathan paused dramatically then added, "I'll tell you what happens. Chaos!"

"You're right," Fergus replied evenly. "And I do have a generator capable of powering the entire resort. Unfortunately, it's been undergoing routine maintenance. The workers assured me they would have everything finished and working before this storm arrived, but obviously that didn't happen. I'm sorry for the inconvenience."

Molly had seen the huge containment vessel for the generator behind a cluster of evergreens out by the parking lot. Knowing Fergus as she did, she could imagine how upset he must be by this situation, but he remained calm, the perfect host even in this imperfect situation.

Jonathan glared at Fergus. "That's what happens when you hire substandard workers."

Fergus's nose twitched but he didn't respond. "There's a smaller backup generator in the basement, and I've switched it on. We will have some inconvenience, but nothing we can't manage."

As Jonathan snorted, Adrian held up a hand. "I know what we can do as we listen to the storm raging out there while we enjoy being nice and cozy in here." He grinned at Fergus. "It'll also help us to not worry about what's beyond our control."

Fergus smiled at his old friend with appreciation. "Be prepared for the outrageous," he warned the room. "He's got that look in his eye."

"Nothing too outrageous," Adrian said. "We can sit on the floor around the fireplace as if we're at camp, and I'll do more Robert Service."

"Not me." Jonathan crossed his arms. "I haven't sat on the floor for years, and I'm not starting now."

Adrian shook his head. "You never were any fun, Hooper."

"Too busy making sure you earn big money, Sinclair."

"Which I appreciate. Still, you're allowed to have fun."

"Making money is fun."

"So is having it," Adrian acknowledged. "But I didn't realize you were such a poor sport."

Jonathan frowned. For some reason, being considered a poor sport apparently bothered him while being a grumpy bully didn't. His eyes narrowed, then he smirked. "I shall remain in my comfortable seat, and you shall consider me as sitting in the balcony, aware but apart. And I bend that much because I respect you." The way he said *respect* seemed to indicate anything but.

With that, the agent leaned his head against the back of the chair and shut his eyes, closing out all he didn't like—which, Molly judged, was pretty much everything and everybody.

"Ever the cooperative spirit, Hooper." Adrian's voice dripped sarcasm. "Thanks."

Jonathan gave a grunt that somehow sounded snooty.

Adrian's irritation with Jonathan was replaced by a twinkle in his eye, the same gleam he got in his movies right before he did something totally unexpected. "I'll just turn the lights off for atmosphere, shall I?" He headed for the wall switch.

Jonathan straightened and glared at him. "You will not."

Adrian paused with a hand on the switch. "Jonathan Hooper, the party pooper."

"Ahem." Fergus held up a hand, stopping the bickering. "Before the show, let me explain the power situation a bit further."

"Is the kitchen powered?" Laura asked, her brow furrowed with concern.

"It's fine." Fergus smiled as her shoulders sagged in relief. "The refrigerators have to be kept cool. However, as I said, your rooms are not on this smaller generator."

Paula made a distressed sound and checked the ceiling as if expecting the roof to collapse on them all.

Jonathan held up his laptop. "What about our electronics? I cannot be without my phone and laptop."

"Charge them here." Fergus gestured toward a nearby outlet.

Paula immediately checked her phone and paled. "I have fifty percent of my battery left, but one bar. Never mind. That one bar disappeared. What happened? It was fine a while ago."

Fergus gave her his best host's smile. "Dense snow like we're getting can interrupt cell service." He shrugged. "Most of the time, all you'll suffer are slower connections and less clear sound."

"Really?" Paula stared at her phone, appearing gobsmacked that it was letting her down.

Trace glanced up from playing with his dog. "Leaves contain lots of water, so they can block signals too. In the woods you might get a signal in winter since there are no leaves, while you might not in summer."

Paula ignored the boy. "How will I talk to Sol?"

"Enjoy the liberation," Jonathan grumbled.

"There's always the possibility that a cell tower will go down under the weight of the ice and snow." Greer seemed pleased with the idea. "Then there's no service, period."

"It's a nightmare." Paula's voice rose. "We're trapped here."

"Classic murder mystery scenario," Jonathan agreed. "Which one of us is the next target?"

Molly frowned. Considering the fact that Adam had been shot earlier and was currently clinging to life—and the shooter was, in fact, at large—she thought Jonathan's comment showed poorer taste than usual. Judging by expressions around the room, she wasn't alone.

Paula's eyes went wide with fright. "You think another of us will be shot?"

"Why not?" Jonathan was enjoying frightening her. He gestured wildly. "He's still lurking out there in a dark hotel, waiting for the right opportunity."

Fergus held up a staying hand. "Enough, Jonathan. Don't worry, Paula. We should be perfectly safe if we don't wander the hotel alone. We've even got our own police officer." He nodded at Greer, who was clearly uncomfortable with the attention. "And Castleglen is prepared for all possibilities." He smiled encouragingly at the attentive expressions. "Chet, help me pass out lanterns and flashlights."

They went to a closet along the side wall and opened the door. Shelves held all kinds of emergency supplies, from blankets and boxes of tissues to rows of flashlights and battery-powered lanterns.

"Everyone gets a flashlight and a lantern," Fergus said. "They have enough power to get you through the night. I'd suggest not using both at the same time if you don't have to. If you want, take a blanket too, though I don't think you'll need it tonight. You probably will by tomorrow since the temperature will drop in the parts of the resort without power."

Fergus handed Paula a sturdy flashlight and a lantern. She eyed them as if she'd never seen such things before.

Molly patted her hand. "Remember, this room will be open all night. You can stay here if you want. Take a sofa and hunker down. There are several outlets so you can charge anything you need, and plenty of blankets to curl up under."

Paula gazed at the fireplace, its glow warm and comforting. "Staying here might not be a bad idea."

Molly noticed that Trace's eyes sparkled in the firelight. Two adventures in the same night—a new dog and a night without electricity. The excitement likely made dealing with the attack on Adam a bit easier.

Molly nudged him with her elbow. "Michigan's not that bad after all, is it?"

He rolled his eyes. "It's still cold."

"Can't argue with that."

By the time everyone had their lights and an extra blanket if they wanted it, Molly was feeling the long day. "Fergus, I'm going to my room."

He gave her shoulders a squeeze. "I'll walk you over, then come back to wrap up a few things."

Laura yawned. "You don't have to. I've had it too. I'll go with Molly."

Paula checked at her watch. "It's too early for bed. It's barely seven o'clock back home."

"We keep baker's hours," Molly said. "Five o'clock this morning was a long time ago."

"You must have gotten up early for your flight here," Laura said to Paula. "Aren't you tired?"

"A bit," Paula admitted. "But I can't go to bed this early, especially when my body knows it's really seven. My mind wouldn't shut off."

Molly smiled. "Stay then. Enjoy the fire. We'll see you at breakfast." She gave a little clap. "Come on, Angus. Time to go to bed."

He blinked himself awake from the cozy spot he'd selected before the fire and trundled over to her. Molly led the way from the bright den down the hall and across the darkened lobby. The only lights were their flashlight beams and the red emergency lighting by doors. The Christmas tree loomed large and black, now menacing in the night. They gave it a wide berth.

"I thought it was weird in this big area earlier with no people," Molly said. "But it's really spooky now with no lights."

"Beware the ghosts of golfers past." Laura made an eerie noise.

"Stop that," Molly protested.

She pulled open the door to the stairwell. Here, the darkness felt even heavier. She swallowed and started up.

"I'm glad we're on the second floor." Laura fell into step behind her as they climbed. "I don't want to be in this stairwell any longer than I have to be."

Their footfalls echoed in the enclosed space. Angus brought up the rear, his toenails tapping a rhythm on the cement stairs. When they emerged in their hallway, they stepped into a long, dark tunnel dimly lit by the red emergency light over the stairwell at their backs.

Molly stared down the hall into the blackness that ate their flashlight beams. A chill crept down her spine. "Creepy."

"Very creepy." Laura aimed her flashlight at the door numbers. "I'm glad our rooms are close to the stairs." She held her key card to her lock, and the door clicked open. "Thank goodness the door locks are battery-operated and still working."

When Laura pushed her door inward, all they could see was blackness with a slightly lighter space at the window, brightened a little by the white snow outside. "See you tomorrow, Molly," she said as she entered the room and set her lantern on the closest table.

Molly turned toward her own room with one last glance down the hall. A quick flash of light caught her eye. "Laura," she hissed. "I saw a light at the end of the hall."

Laura was at her side in a moment, peering into the darkness. "There's nothing there."

"There was."

"Are you sure? Maybe your flashlight simply reflected off something."

Molly knew what she'd seen. "It was a burst of light where there shouldn't be any."

Laura checked all around. "Did anyone else come up to bed?"

"Nope." Molly headed down the hall, her flashlight making a circle of brightness ahead of her. Angus trotted beside her, his ears and eyebrows at attention.

Laura was right behind them. "This is when creepy becomes scary."

The rapid beat of Molly's heart sounded an agreement.

"Slow down." Laura pulled on Molly's arm. "What if it's the shooter?"

Molly stopped, feeling a chill at the thought of him, then shook her head. "No. If he wanted to shoot us, he'd have done so already. He doesn't want us. If he's still here, he wants Rocky. I'm thinking this guy is the photographer, Lou Duckworth."

Laura stepped closer to Molly. "And I'm betting Duckworth doesn't want to be found either. What if he's waiting around the corner, ready to grab us?"

Molly pondered that idea. "No, he's not. Because there are *two of us and one of him.*" She said the last so loudly that Angus peered up at her in surprise. She smiled down at him. "Just scaring away bad guys, buddy."

Laura snorted. "I'm sure he's running for his life."

"He should be if he's got any smarts."

With renewed resolve, Molly continued down the hall, Laura beside her. They reached the T intersection at the end.

"Was the light to the right or the left?" Laura asked.

"I couldn't tell."

Molly peeked cautiously around the corner to the right, Laura to the left. Another corridor black with shadows stretched both ways. Molly felt both disappointed and relieved when they found nothing.

"Come on." Molly went right and started down the hall, pushing on each door as she went.

"Do you expect one to open for you?" Laura asked.

"No, but you never know. He could have checked in before we knew he was here. Before the staff left. Before the storm."

"Could be. But then he'd have a key card, and his door would be locked tight. We could be walking right past him."

Molly considered that as she continued trying doors. "Probably, but let's think creatively. You know how they tape doors open in detective shows? Maybe our guy did that. He didn't register because he didn't want a record of his presence after his legal issues with Rocky. He strolled in like he belonged, and anyone who saw him assumed he was a guest. He wandered until he found someone cleaning a room. While the cleaner was occupied with the bed or the bathroom, he taped the door. He waited for her to leave, then moved in and made himself comfortable."

"You don't think that's a bit of a stretch?"

Molly raised an eyebrow at her friend. They'd been involved in solving more than one mystery together. "In my experience, nothing is a stretch."

"Valid point," Laura said. "Fine, say you're right and he sneaked in like you think. What would you do if a door you pushed on did open?"

Molly had to laugh. "Probably scream in shock."

"We've got a shooter and a photographer. I wonder which one we'd find."

"I know my preference."

The words were barely out of her mouth when the door of room 254 glided silently open under Molly's hand.

10

Molly squeaked as she lost her balance and pitched headfirst into the room. She scrabbled to keep her footing and ended up on one knee.

"Holy cow!" Laura held the door so it wouldn't close on Molly, then aimed her flashlight into the dark room. It appeared empty of life.

Molly got to her feet and added her flashlight beam to Laura's. The room appeared similar to hers, the main difference being that the colors were soft grays and blues.

"Pretty," Laura said.

"Yeah, but how did this door open?" Molly aimed her light at the door. "Tape. I was right."

Laura laughed. "Aren't you the smart one."

"Don't you forget it."

Molly examined the strip of duct tape that prevented the bolt from engaging, rendering the lock useless. It had been placed carefully, so that none of the tape overlapped to the outside of the door. Anyone passing would never know the lock had been tampered with. Whoever was using this room obviously wanted privacy and secrecy.

Laura ran her light around the room. "It's the photographer."

Sitting on the bureau was a duffel with a pair of cameras visible inside. Another duffel sat on a chair, a dark sweater and a single black sock sticking out of the unzipped top. The bed was still made, but someone had obviously sat on it, rumpling its covers.

"We've got to tell Fergus." Molly retreated to the hall.

"And Greer."

Molly used the bottom of her sweater to grab the doorknob and pull the door shut. "Fingerprints," she explained, then gave a push to make sure it opened again.

Angus ran beside them down the hall, uncertain what was going on but enjoying the excitement. They hit the stairwell and hurried down. Molly's breath came quickly, and she felt like she was being zapped with low-voltage electricity. There was such satisfaction in helping solve a mystery.

She and Laura burst into the den. "We found him!"

Startled faces turned their way. "What? Who?"

"The photographer," Laura replied triumphantly with a huge grin.

"Not the photographer himself, but his room," Molly clarified. "He taped the door so it wouldn't latch."

Fergus gestured to Molly. "Show me."

Greer jumped up from the couch where she had been sitting with Rocky. "Let's go."

Molly led the way back up the stairs and down the hall. She felt like a tour guide, thanks to the parade of curious people behind her. Even Jonathan had gotten up to follow her and Laura. She reached the room and shined the light on the door. "254. This is it."

Fergus inspected the door. "I don't see the tape."

"You won't," Molly said. "He's been very careful not to be noticed."

"I wonder why," Rocky said drily.

Greer held out a hand to stop Fergus as he reached for the handle. "Let me." She pulled on a pair of gloves and carefully pushed on the door. Nothing happened. "You sure this is the right room?"

"Positive," Molly replied.

"This is it." Laura indicated the door number. "254."

"And it slid open when you touched it?" Greer asked.

"It did." Molly insisted. "The tape stopped the lock from engaging."

Greer shoved harder this time. Still nothing. She gripped the handle and jiggled it. "You may have gotten in, Molly, but we aren't going to. It's locked, like it should be."

A chill slid down Molly's back. "He was watching us."

"Had to be." Laura rubbed her hands up and down her arms as if warming herself.

Trent moved to stand beside her as if for protection.

Everyone shined their flashlights up and down the hall. Nothing. They all huddled closer for safety and comfort.

"Here." Fergus held out a rectangular plastic card. "Master key."

Greer indicated the door. "Go ahead."

Fergus swiped and the door clicked open.

Everyone moved as if to enter the room, but Greer held up a hand. "Stay back."

Reluctantly, they stepped away, and Greer disappeared into the room, her hand on the weapon sitting on her hip. She reappeared almost immediately.

"Empty." She pulled the door firmly closed. "I'll come back tomorrow when there's some daylight to search more thoroughly. He may have inadvertently left something in his haste." She eyed Molly and Laura. "How did you know it was the photographer's room?"

"A duffel of cameras sat on the bureau," Molly said with a shudder. The whole situation was so creepy. As soon as she and Laura had left, he must have grabbed his things and gone—but where? He certainly hadn't left the hotel, not on a night like this. As if to reinforce that thought, the building creaked and a draft of cold air raced down the hall.

"How did he know you two were here?" Greer asked.

"He probably heard us," Molly said. "We weren't trying to be quiet."

"And we were using our flashlights," Laura added.

"How did you know he was here?" Greer asked.

"I saw a light, and we went to check it out," Molly explained.

Greer frowned, likely disapproving of them investigating. "Can you describe the light?"

"It was more like a flash," Molly said. "It wasn't constant like a beam would be. It was as if he ducked around the corner and flicked his light off as soon as he saw our lights."

Greer glanced up and down the hall, appearing thoughtful. "He came out of his room. He walked to the end of the hall and went toward the stairwell that would take him down toward the den. Toward people. Toward Rocky." Her voice soured. "Toward another picture."

In spite of the seriousness of the moment, Molly had to bite back a smile at Greer's expression.

"He had barely rounded the corner when he heard you two," the officer continued. "He shut his light off immediately, and then when you started toward him, he hustled back the way he'd come."

"But where did he go?" Molly voiced what they must all be thinking. "All the doors are locked."

"Except the far stairwell." Greer pointed to the end of the hall they stood in. A red *EXIT* glowed over a door.

"Up or down?" Rocky asked, regarding Greer with fascination as she played out what sounded like a reasonable and probable course of events.

She shook her head. "Who knows? If he's after you, Rocky, he could have gone either way. You were downstairs in the den, but your room is upstairs. Then again, more pictures could be the last thing on his mind. He could simply want to find a place to hide."

"Do we launch a search?" Trace's voice was full of excitement. He still carried his pup, who had settled against him as if he planned to stay there forever.

Fergus shook his head. "There are a hundred guest rooms and suites in this building, plus the restaurants, offices, and other operations centers. The laundry and trash facilities alone offer endless hiding places. Trying to find him at night with no electricity in most of the building would be an exercise in futility. Even seeking him in daylight with the few of us searching would be useless. He can simply keep moving ahead, circling back, hustling up or down as needed."

Rocky made a disgusted noise. "Nobody ever said Lou Duckworth was stupid."

Now that there was no more excitement, Jonathan, Chet, and Paula made their way back toward the den. Bobby schlepped along behind like a reluctant caboose, checking over his shoulder to likely see if Greer was coming too. Carol and Harvey waved good night and went to their room.

Greer turned to Molly and Laura. "You didn't happen to see if there was any sign of a weapon, did you?"

"You think Duckworth is the shooter?" Rocky shook his head. "He's a parasite, but I don't think he'd shoot anyone. I don't think he's brave enough."

"Tell me more about him," Greer said. "I need to figure out how he thinks."

"Of course." Rocky gave her his complete attention. "Anything I can do to help."

Something about Rocky's intense agreement must have impressed Greer, because she gave him the first genuine smile Molly had seen on her face since she'd arrived. The officer started into the stairwell, Rocky on her heels.

Fergus stopped with Molly at her door as she fought a yawn. "Are you going to be all right?"

Molly gave a small grin. "And if I say no?"

"I'll sleep outside your door all night so no one can get in."

"That's a very generous offer, but I'm afraid your back would be mighty sore tomorrow."

"Maybe," he said, "but you'll be safe." He took her hands and gave her that special smile. "That's what counts."

Her heart melted at his concern. "No need to injure yourself to be my knight in shining armor. You need to be in top form for the day ahead. But thank you."

"My room's right across the hall from yours. If you need something in the night, come get me. Right now, I need to do a final check of the place. I also want to make a call to check on Adam's condition."

She heard not only the concern but the sense of responsibility in his words. "It wasn't your fault, Fergus."

"It happened at my resort."

She gave him a hug, knowing nothing but Adam's complete recovery would comfort him. "Let me know if there's a change, good or bad."

"Will do." After giving Angus a quick pat on the head, Fergus disappeared through the stairwell door. Trent said good night to Laura and went into his room. With a wave to Molly, Laura squared her shoulders and entered hers.

Suddenly, the hall was all shadows and threat. Thinking of the black void that was her room made Molly wrap her arms around her body protectively. The idea of a night alone in this huge, creaky building unnerved her. She told herself she was being a wimp and needed to buck up. She needed to find that fine line between being cautious about the dangers and falling victim to needless anxiety and fear.

A door in the stairwell at her back slammed shut on another floor, making her jump. Upstairs or down? She couldn't tell. Was it Lou Duckworth or the shooter?

Footsteps echoed on the stairs, coming closer and closer. She stared at the door, which was eerie in the red light over it. Her mouth went dry, her breathing shallow. Her heart raced in her chest.

The bar on the door clanged as someone pushed it from the other side. The door began to open. Molly made a little whimpering sound, embarrassing herself even though no one could hear.

The door flew wide, and Harvey stepped through, a mug in each hand. Molly's knees went weak with relief. "Harvey. I wasn't expecting to see you."

"I ducked back downstairs for a bit." He held up a mug. "Carol wanted a cup of chamomile tea to help her sleep."

Molly realized she must have not noticed him, busy talking to the others. She took a deep breath. Her heart rate began its descent to normal.

"Remind her how wonderful I am on the days she's miffed at me, would you?" He stopped in front of his room.

Remembering his full hands, Molly hurried over and knocked for him.

"Carol, it's me," he called.

The door opened and Carol appeared, swathed head to toe in the plush robe that came in every room. "Ah, there's my room service," she said with a smile.

"Your tea, madam," Harvey said, returning her grin as he entered the room.

Molly quickly bid them good night again and returned to her own door. She held her key card to her lock, and when it clicked, she pushed the door open.

It was as if the darkness inside reached out to catch her.

Her smile disappeared. Angus sat beside her, staring unhappily into the room. She shined her flashlight, but its beam seemed to bounce back without illuminating anything.

She retreated a step into the hall, and the door closed. She gave herself a little shake. At this rate, she'd be spending the night on her threshold instead of Fergus. Or taking refuge in the den with Paula.

She stared down the black tunnel of the hall. The flashlight beam lit the walls but not the small alcove into which each door was set.

Anyone could be hiding in those little nooks.

She glanced over her shoulder at the stairwell, then she eyed the 202 in front of her. Black and empty behind a locked door was better than black and empty in an exposed hall or open stairwell, waiting for someone to grab her.

Then she thought of something better than either option.

She knocked on Laura's door. When Laura answered, Molly grinned and announced, "Sleepover!"

Laura raised an eyebrow. "Scared of being alone in this big, dark place with two shooters wandering around?"

Molly made a face. "I don't know if 'scared' is the right word, but I sure don't like it. Therefore, Angus and I invite you to a sleepover."

"Let me get my stuff and I'll be right over."

Twenty minutes later, Molly and Laura sat in the huge king-size bed, pillows bunched behind them, Angus cuddled contentedly between them.

"I'm going to read for a few minutes," Molly said. "Will the light from my e-reader bother you?"

"Not at all." Laura covered a yawn. "I set my alarm for seven."

Molly chuckled. "We're sleeping in."

"Might as well—if we can. Habit is about to clash with hope." Laura slid down, fluffed her pillow a few times, and closed her eyes.

Angus crawled up the covers until he was almost lying on Molly's pillow. He lifted his bright little eyes to her, beseeching. She knew exactly what he wanted.

"Okay." She raised the covers, and Angus didn't hesitate. He burrowed under the covers and pressed his body against Molly's. She put her e-reader on the night table and nestled in herself.

She had just closed her eyes when a fresh wave of dread forced them open. She gently extricated herself from the covers and crept to the door, where she saw that she'd been right. They'd forgotten to engage the security latch. She quickly flipped the metal bar over the catch, then double-checked the dead bolt. They were safe from bad guys now, at least for the night.

Tomorrow was another story.

11

Laura's alarm wakened them to a room still mostly dark, but with dim light seeping around the curtains. At least Molly could see well enough that she wouldn't need to use her flashlight. She pushed herself to sitting, taking care to keep the covers draped over her shoulders. Her nose was cold. She blew out a puff of air, expecting to see a condensate cloud before her. Fortunately it wasn't that chilly yet.

"You're letting cold air in," Laura muttered from her side of the great bed.

"Sorry." Molly climbed from the bed and adjusted the covers so no cold air found its way under.

Laura hummed contentedly.

Molly pulled on a sweater over her pajamas, then the giant robe, hood and all. She padded over the rug to throw back the curtains.

She stared. In all the years she'd spent in the Upper Peninsula, she'd never seen anything like this. The storm snarled, the wind whipped, and the snow swirled. The entire world was white.

It was hard to believe that somewhere south of them, the sun shone. Somewhere, people were having picnics and frolicking in the ocean. In Australia it was summer.

Laura, wrapped in her own spa robe, came to stand beside her. "Whiteout."

After brushing their teeth and changing into fresh clothes, they left their room and went down to the first floor. Molly detoured to the front entrance and the protection of the canopied awning for Angus to visit the outdoors without being lost in the snow. They bumped into Trace with his pup doing the same thing.

"How'd he do during the night?" Molly gave the pup a scratch around his floppy ears.

"He was such a brave boy, weren't you, Hero?" Trace gave the dog such a loving gaze that Molly couldn't help but smile.

"So his name's Hero?"

"That's right. Because he is one. He survived alone in that storm like some superhero."

"He's definitely a survivor, and a lucky boy that you saw him."

"I'm the lucky one." Trace gave a gentle tug on the rope he was using as a leash. "Time to go in, Hero."

He took one step toward the door, and Hero dashed past him, Angus on his tail. Molly hurried after the dogs.

"I'm so glad Rocky didn't try to go to the hospital with Adam," Trace said as they hustled inside. "I mean, I feel bad he's alone and all, but Rocky would be stuck there until the storm was over."

"Your brother definitely made the best choice," Molly agreed. "Any word on how Adam's doing?"

"Rocky won't say it to me, but I think it's bad." Trace bent to brush some snow off Hero's nose. "He called the doctor a little while ago, and they were talking about . . ." The boy's voice hitched. "End-of-life stuff."

Molly's heart squeezed. Would Adam soon be a murder victim? "I'm sorry. I know he's a friend to all of you."

"It's scary. And it doesn't make sense. I mean, who'd want to hurt Adam?"

With a shake of his head, Trace headed back to the Sinclairs' suite with Hero while Molly moved toward the den, Angus at her heels. She was going to let him stay warm by the fire while she worked on breakfast.

She pushed the door open and stopped. Huddled on a couch beneath a blue blanket lay Paula, her gorgeous fall of hair in a braid that tumbled over the edge of the blanket. Angus hurried over, stood on his hind legs, and planted his front paws on the couch to get a good look.

The door thudded closed behind Molly, waking Paula. She gasped when she saw Angus mere inches away. She sat up, blinking, her eyes wide, her hand going to her heart.

Molly held out her hands. "Sorry. We didn't mean to startle you. Down, Angus."

He lowered to the floor obediently, but gave a little woof of greeting.

"And hello to you." Paula reached down and gave him a scratch, then swung her feet to the floor. "What time is it?"

"Half past seven," Molly answered. "Did you sleep here all night?"

"I did. With lights—which I kept on—and heat and a bathroom just down the hall. I figured if I could see, I was safe."

Molly decided not to mention that Adam could see when he was shot. If Paula's reasoning got her through the night, she wasn't going to poke holes in it.

Paula stood and folded her blanket. "There was no way I was going up to that room by myself." She shivered at the thought. "I don't know how you stood it."

Molly gave a little shrug. "Sleepover. Laura joined Angus and me."

Paula rubbed an eye. "I was the only girl up on our floor. No one to bunk with. Except for Greer, and she slept in that room connected to the Sinclairs' suite. Gotta protect Rocky, you know."

Molly ignored the acidic tone of that comment. "Laura, Carol, and I are about to prep breakfast. Want to help?"

Paula pulled on her aqua boots. "Me? In the kitchen?"

"Sure. You can cut fruit."

Paula thought for a minute. "I guess I can't ruin a banana."

Molly noted what was needed for the coffee bar, then they made their way to the kitchen where Laura was sautéing a pan of onions while Carol slid a fragrant coffee cake out of the oven.

"Paula's come to help," Molly announced, and Paula smiled at the shower of welcomes sent her way. For the first time since she'd arrived, her shoulders seemed to relax.

Soon, a chafing dish of scrambled eggs laced with ham, cheese, and onion sat ready to go beside the coffee cake. A large tureen of apples, bananas, and oranges studded with purple and green grapes rested on the counter, Paula standing proudly beside it. Yogurt and granola finished off the selections.

Molly quickly got the buffet tables ready to go and carried the food out. The scent of the coffee cake drew the first few diners. By the time the first group retreated to the den with full plates, the rest had appeared.

Everyone tucked in eagerly, with little conversation. *Cold weather makes you hungry*, Molly mused as she ate a bite of eggs.

Cleanup was quick and easy with Harvey, Trent, and Chet pitching in. Paula watched, fascinated, but made no move to help. Molly decided the woman honestly didn't know what to do. From her expression, she'd never seen men working in a kitchen before.

"Did you grow up with household staff, Paula?" Molly asked as she and Laura tackled dishes.

Paula scrunched up her face. "It's embarrassing to admit, but yes. My parents are really rich. I never did anything in the kitchen before today." She held up her hands. "I know, it's almost shameful in this day and age. But it's not my fault my father's a studio executive and my mom's one of the premier acting coaches in Hollywood."

"I give you credit for having your own job instead of sponging off them," Molly said.

Paula smiled at the compliment. "This PR job isn't my first, and I don't want to fail this time. Sol never cuts me any slack, regardless of the fact that my father is a Hollywood heavy hitter."

"It's never too late to learn important things, like how to cut fruit," Molly said. "You're now part of the cook team. You will leave Loch Mallaig with genuine life skills."

"And they will include taking out the garbage," Carol said, pushing a tied trash bag into Paula's hands. She grabbed another. "Follow me."

Paula grinned from ear to ear and obeyed.

Laura hung up her dish towel. "I'm going to the gym to use the treadmill."

"I need some movement too," Molly said. "Let me do a final check on the coffee bar and I'll join you."

She walked into the den with Paula as Trace burst into laughter and held out his phone. "I'm getting service for the moment, and oh ho, Rocky! You and Greer are getting more attention."

"Great." Greer growled her displeasure. "I don't want to know what they're saying. Last night was bad enough."

"Oh, you'll want to see this," Trace assured her. "It's a new picture."

"A new picture?" Greer appeared both angry and intrigued. "How? Where?"

Trace turned his phone toward her. "It's a good picture."

She snatched it and stared. "How did he get that shot?"

Paula pulled up the site on her laptop. "Greer, this is a great photo of you. You're gorgeous." She was practically rubbing her hands with delight at the new surge of PR.

Molly peered over Paula's shoulder to view the image. The picture had been taken in the hall outside room 254, the door number clear in the background. Greer was grinning at Rocky, her face alight. With soft eyes and a goofy smile, Rocky appeared to be completely smitten. The caption read, *Rocky's got it bad.*

Rocky examined the picture, his expression a study in disbelief as he saw himself portrayed as a lovestruck fool.

Greer stood with her head down, eyes closed, and fingers pressed to her forehead as if in pain. "This is so embarrassing."

"Agreed," Rocky said. "I look like an idiot."

"You do." Trace laughed. "Your mouth's hanging open and everything."

"It is not." Rocky leaned in. "Is it?"

"Might as well be," Trace teased.

Greer groaned, and Rocky quietly asked her, "You okay?"

She shrugged but still wouldn't meet his eyes. "How did Duckworth take that? Where was he?"

"Probably in the indent of a door down the hall," Rocky said. "Lost in the shadows."

"I am going to figure out which door," Greer said. "Then I'm going to find him and take him and his blasted camera into police custody."

"I'm coming with you." Rocky was at her side in an instant.

"I'm fine," Greer protested. "You don't need to come."

"I know," Rocky replied, "but you shouldn't be wandering around by yourself."

She glared at him. "I can take care of myself."

He held up a hand. "I don't doubt that for a minute, but I'm coming. Someone in this building has a gun and has used it."

"I'll come with you, Greer." Bobby got to his feet.

Molly met Fergus's gaze from across the room. Poor Bobby. He hadn't had a chance before Rocky showed up, and he certainly didn't have one now.

"I'm coming too." Trace stood, Hero in his arms. "Where Rocky goes, I go too."

Greer held up a hand. "No. No one but Rocky." She shot Bobby an apologetic glance. "And that's only because I have orders from the chief to keep him with me. But no one else. I don't want people contaminating any evidence or getting hurt."

Bobby sagged in defeat and sat.

"I'd never contaminate anything." Trace sounded insulted.

"Then you have to leave the dog," Greer said. "He'd slobber all over everything."

"He would not," Trace argued.

"Of course he would."

Hero gave the boy huge puppy-dog eyes. With a sigh, Trace conceded. "He would." He plopped on a love seat and Hero settled in his lap.

As Rocky and Greer left the room, Molly checked the creamers, the sweeteners, and the tea options, especially the peppermint. All was good.

Fergus met her at the door. "What are you up to?"

"I'm going to join Laura in the gym," she told him.

"Have fun," he said.

Molly chuckled. "I'm excited for the hot shower after the workout more than the workout itself. I'm glad the hot water heaters in this section of the building are still working."

He gave her shoulders a quick squeeze. "Shows how smart you are."

Molly felt warm and toasty as she made her way to the locker room. Somehow Fergus always knew what to say to make her feel special.

When Molly entered the gym, Laura was already on a treadmill, Adrian and Trent were playing basketball, and Chet was working with Trace at the weight machines.

Hero lay by the door, his leash tethering him to the sign-in desk to keep him safely out of the way. Angus walked to him and lay down.

Both dogs rested their chins on their front paws and observed the foolish humans wearing themselves out when they could be laying around enjoying life.

Molly went to the treadmill beside Laura and selected an old *I Love Lucy* rerun to watch on the small screen as she worked out. Halfway through the episode, Greer and Rocky entered the gym, both wearing workout clothes. Rocky went to the weights while Greer headed for the treadmill next to Molly.

"How's it going over here?" Rocky asked Chet and Trace.

"I want to do the free weights," Trace groused as he did leg lifts on a machine.

"We'll get there," Chet assured Trace, then told Rocky, "He's doing great."

Molly smiled, unable to help finding Trace's youthful attitude amusing. Her mirth faded at Greer's serious expression. "I take it you didn't find anything upstairs?"

Greer shook her head. "Not that I expected to." She peeked inside her tote and frowned. "I forgot a water bottle. I'm going to grab one from the kitchen."

While Greer was gone, Trace finally reached the free weights. He, Chet, and Rocky debated what the boy's starting weight should be. Chet and Rocky suggested a lower amount, which could always be increased. Trace, with visions of grandeur, wanted to begin with an overly optimistic amount.

Suppressing another grin, Molly returned her attention to the small screen on her treadmill, where Lucy was stashing chocolates down her dress and in her hat.

Movement caught Molly's eye. Someone had pushed the locker room door open a few inches. As if in slow motion, the barrel of a gun appeared.

"Gun!" she screamed, and the crack of a shot cut the air.

12

Molly threw herself from the treadmill, and the change from the moving belt to the stationary floor brought her to her knees. As she struggled to her feet, tripping over herself in her hurry, she saw the locker room door glide shut once more.

Laura dismounted from her treadmill more successfully than Molly and raced to where the men were huddled around the free weights. "Are you all right?" she asked. "Is anyone hurt?"

Molly, finally gaining her feet, made for the locker room door. She had to hurry or the shooter would get away—again. She gave a quick glance at the scrum of people by the weights but couldn't tell if anyone was hurt or not. Was someone trying to murder Rocky again? Why?

Questions burned in her mind as she burst through the door and ran into the hall. On the left was Chet's office, its door propped open. To the right were the men's and women's locker rooms. On the floor in the middle of the hall lay a figure curled in on himself as if he had a stomachache. He wore shorts and a sleeveless shirt, and his freckled skin was white with shock.

"Bobby!"

Molly rushed to him as he patted wildly at his stomach. Had he been shot? Had there been a second explosion of sound that she'd somehow missed? She dropped to her knees beside him as he brought his hands to his face and whimpered.

"Bobby?" She reached for his hand. "Where are you hurt?"

He groaned.

"Let me see." She tried to pull his hands away.

At first he resisted, but then he let her see the great lump growing on his forehead, the skin red and scraped but not bleeding. A huge bruise was already forming.

As she evaluated Bobby, she worried about what was happening in the gym. Had anyone been hurt out there? *Concentrate, Molly.* Bobby needed her here.

"Did the shooter hit you?" she asked. Poor guy. He'd been in the wrong place at the wrong time.

"I-I guess so," he managed in a strangled voice, which broke on a sob. "It all happened so fast. It's all a b-blur."

"I bet." She patted his shoulder to soothe him. "Can you sit up? Do you feel dizzy?" She was concerned about a concussion.

Slowly Bobby uncurled, rolling over onto his hands and knees. He stopped there, letting his head hang. "Ow! It hurts."

"I'm so sorry." She patted his back. Where was Greer? She'd know what to do.

He leaned back on his bent knees and wrapped his arms about his body. He swayed a bit.

"Did you hurt your stomach?" Molly envisioned a punch to the solar plexus.

"No. Just my head." He placed one foot on the floor, ready to push himself upright, but he stalled, unable to go further. He shut his eyes, and Molly suspected he was in great pain.

"Chet must have cold packs in his office," Molly said. "Let me get you one to stop the swelling."

Bobby made an inarticulate sound.

Molly scrambled to her feet and hurried to Chet's office. She was scanning her surroundings and wondering where to find an ice pack, when Chet charged through the door from the gym. He stopped abruptly in the hallway, likely halted by the sight of Bobby.

Molly rushed back into the hall. "The shooter struck him." She gestured toward Bobby, now sitting against the wall, elbows on knees, head in his hands. "He's got a lump on his forehead. Do you have any cold packs?"

"You bet." Chet hurried past Molly to a small refrigerator in the corner of his office. Molly left the doorway and took a seat beside Bobby. She was worried about him. He wasn't the superhero type.

"You're going to be okay." She patted his arm.

Suddenly the hall was full of people as Laura, Rocky, Trace, and Trent burst in. Molly let out a relieved breath when she saw all the men moving easily.

"Whoever the shooter is," she muttered to Bobby, "he has terrible aim. He missed everyone."

"Everyone but me," Bobby grumbled, and Molly gave his shoulder a consoling pat.

Greer raced into the hall. "Rocky?"

He waved at her. "Here."

She steadied herself with a hand against the wall. "Thank goodness."

Rocky reached her side and squeezed her shoulder. "It's all right. I'm fine."

She peered into his eyes, her own skin pale and stricken. "I left you. I didn't do my duty."

Rocky lifted her chin. "It's okay."

She shook her head. "It's not okay." She took a deep breath, straightened her shoulders, and dropped down beside Bobby. "Tell me what happened, Bobby."

Bobby was obviously in pain, but he seemed intent on appearing brave now that Greer was beside him. "It's all one big blur." He drew a wobbly hand through the air, indicating his movements. "I came out of the men's locker room, and there he was. I didn't have time to do anything."

"Before or after the shot?" Greer asked.

Bobby's expression was blank.

She gave up, openly disappointed he had no more to add. "Come on. Let's get you to the den where you can lie down."

"What if he's still in the men's locker room?" Trace asked. Molly noticed that his eyes were alight with excitement, not fear or distress. He grabbed the door, threw it open, and disappeared inside before anyone could stop him.

Rocky grabbed the door swishing shut and leaned in. "Trace, get back here!"

"Don't worry," Greer said. "The shooter's long gone. Trace will be fine."

"But he might be contaminating the crime scene."

Greer blinked in surprise, grinned, and shook her head. "Any clues that might have been in there or out here have well and truly disappeared."

Trace reappeared, wearing an air of disappointment. "No one in there."

A pitiful canine whine leaked into the silence.

Trace's eyes went wide. "How could I forget Hero?" He raced back into the gym.

"Got to love thirteen-year-olds," Rocky said as he helped Bobby to his feet. He kept his hand on Bobby's elbow until the man was steady on his feet. Then he and Greer led him through the gym, where Trace was on his knees apologizing to Hero. The dog clearly held no grudges, as he was covering the boy's face with kisses of forgiveness.

Angus sat beside Hero watching the show. When he saw Molly, his ears perked up and his tail thumped on the floor.

"Good boy, Angus." Molly rubbed his head. "Come." Together they followed the procession to the den.

Rocky helped Bobby lie down on one of the couches. Greer covered him with a blanket and placed a cold pack she'd gotten from Chet on his forehead.

Adrian surveyed the proceedings with concern while Paula peered over the crowd, trying to see what was going on. "Ice for a bump like that is good," she said with an astonishing authority that immediately faltered with her next words. "Or-or that's what I've heard."

Molly made a cup of tea and added a couple teaspoons of sugar. She took it to Bobby. "Here. Drink this."

He grimaced. "I don't like tea."

"Drink it." Greer knelt beside him. "The sugar will help stave off shock." When Bobby eyed her skeptically, she smiled at him. "Please?"

He flushed and took a sip.

"All of it," Greer pressed.

When he was finished, she took the cup and stood. He grabbed her hand. "Don't leave me. What if he comes back? What if he thinks I can identify him? I'm the one who needs you now."

Laura, standing beside Molly, leaned in and whispered in her ear, "The man never misses an opportunity to sell something. He's almost down for the count, yet he's still trying to sell himself to the girl."

"Poor guy. It's one sale that's not going through."

"Too true."

Greer disentangled her hand from Bobby's grip. "I think you're fine here, Bobby. You've got a room full of bodyguards." She indicated all the people watching them. "I've got to go investigate what's left of the scene. I need to find out who did this to you." Her smile at him was sweet but impersonal.

Bobby followed her with his eyes as she left the room. His expression was so full of yearning it made Molly sad. When the door closed behind her, he closed his eyes. "I need a painkiller."

"There's some in a first aid station in the gym," Chet said.

"I'll get it," Molly offered. She left Angus and the others in the den. She caught up to Greer outside the gym and remembered she had more information to share. "I saw the gun," Molly told the officer. "I was on the treadmill, and I spotted the barrel sticking out of the locker room door. I warned everyone, but I fell as I jumped from the treadmill. I picked myself up and while everyone ran toward the men, I ran toward the gun and found Bobby on the floor."

"Show me," Greer ordered.

Molly led the way across the gym to the door to the locker rooms. "He's missed twice."

"It's harder to hit a moving person across a room than most people know," Greer said. "Why do you think all those innocent bystanders get hurt while the target walks away?" She appraised the gym as they went. "Rocky, Trace, and Chet were all constantly moving, adjusting weights, getting new weights, and spotting Trace, right?"

"Right," Molly confirmed as they paused outside the door the shooter had aimed through.

"Show me where the gun was when you saw it," Greer said.

Molly put her hand in the air where the gun barrel had been. "Right about here."

"And it was aimed at the men?"

"As far as I could tell."

Greer strode across the room and studied the wall behind where the men had been. "Aha!"

Molly joined her and saw the bullet embedded in the wall. "Think it'll match the one they took from Adam?"

"I'd be very surprised if it didn't. Could you go to Fergus's office and get me a piece of paper and some tape? We are not touching this. The state police forensics team will take care of it." Greer glanced at the snow whirling and writhing outside the windows. "After the storm."

Molly hurried to Fergus's office, got an index card, a pen, and some tape from the desk, and returned to Greer. The officer noted the time and date and added her initials to the card. She placed it over the bullet hole in the wall and secured it with several layers of tape.

"That should do it," Greer said. "Now show me where you found Bobby."

They reached the hall, and Molly showed Greer to the right spot. "He was curled up right there, near the men's locker room door."

"So Bobby comes out of the locker room at the same time the shooter plans to run in there," Greer said. "They meet. Bobby goes down. The shooter keeps running into the locker room." She grabbed the door handle and pulled. "Anyone in here? Women coming in."

There was no response—not that Molly expected any—so they entered.

Greer strode ahead. "I know he's not here any longer, but I need to figure out where he went from here."

As the door slid shut behind them, Molly saw something caught under its bottom edge, sliding with the door as it moved. At first, she thought it was a piece of trash, but that seemed unlikely in this immaculately kept resort. She bent to see more clearly and realized the object was a thin latex glove rolled in on itself. It was the kind doctors and nurses might wear—and the kind a shooter might wear to protect himself from leaving fingerprints or picking up gunshot residue. "Greer."

Greer joined Molly and grinned when she saw the glove. "What have we here?" She snapped a photo of the glove. She slid her phone back in her pocket and picked up the glove with the pen she'd pocketed.

She slid it into a plastic evidence bag she pulled from her tote, giving a surprised Molly a shrug to acknowledge she always came prepared. She sealed, dated, and initialed it and slid it in her bag. "The state lab will look for DNA."

"Too bad they can't get it for a couple of days."

"Nothing we can do about that. But we know now that he escaped through here." Greer strode through the room, past the lockers. "There's got to be another door somewhere or he'd have trapped himself."

"Or herself," Molly added.

"Or herself." Greer's voice echoed in the empty room as she moved farther from the door and around a corner. "Hey, there's a back door here."

Molly grimaced. "You don't think the shooter went outside in this weather, do you?" Instead of a response, she heard the door open, then close, then nothing. "Greer? Greer! You can't go outside by yourself." She had started after the officer when the door banged open again.

"He definitely went that way," Greer reported. "There's a short corridor out there with four other doors. One opens to the ladies' locker room. One opens to the pool area. The third opens to stairs that lead into the basement. And the last is the door to the outside."

"You don't think he circled back through the ladies' locker room, do you?" Molly asked.

"I don't. What if one of us had been in there?"

"So the basement?"

"Well, he's not likely going outside in this weather. The basement's the perfect hiding place. I'll search it after I talk with Fergus about what's down there."

"Don't go down by yourself."

"Right. I'll take Rocky along. I'm not crazy about the idea of possibly taking him into danger, but he's safer with me than he is out of my sight apparently." Greer wandered down every aisle of the locker room, opening each locker as she went.

Molly continued to study the main locker room door, trying to think like the shooter. As he escaped, he wouldn't want to take the time to pull the door open, would he? It was a heavy door that required users to stop and pull. Those few seconds would make him vulnerable to discovery. Wouldn't he prepare his escape route ahead of time?

She dropped to her knees and searched under the lockers, and there it was. "Greer, I found something," she called.

Greer hurried to her and dropped down. Using her trusty pen, she coaxed a wedge of wood out from under the locker.

"He propped open the door," Molly said.

"That's smart. Just kick the wedge out of the way and the door closes behind you." She grinned at Molly. "Nice work."

Greer bagged and tagged the wedge and added it to the collection in her bag, and then they prepared to leave.

Rocky met up with them by the door. "I've been searching for you," he told Greer with a grin. "You're falling down on your bodyguard duties, and I feel unsafe."

Greer suddenly looked distressed. "Why would you want my protection? I failed to protect you from being shot at again."

Rocky scrutinized her. Greer flushed and shifted from foot to foot. Then he gave that smile that lit the silver screen. "I'm not complaining. Why would I? I'm lucky enough to have a beautiful bodyguard. And I'm not shot. Now tell me what you've found." He pointed to her bag.

"All right."

Rocky stepped close, and Molly saw the officer bite her lip. She suppressed a smile. Gone was the disdain Greer had originally felt for the man. Now she was falling under his spell, and if Molly wasn't mistaken, Rocky was equally taken with her.

Molly slipped away, heading for the den, grinning at her unrealistic dreams of a romance between a Hollywood icon and a small-town cop. It would make a great movie, but the possibilities of Greer getting hurt were high when he went back to California. But what if he really moved here?

She was so lost in plotting Greer's romance she almost bumped into Jonathan glaring at the empty serving tables.

"Where is the food?" he growled. "There's supposed to be food."

Molly checked her watch. "It's not quite time for lunch yet."

"You said you'd feed us breakfast."

"We did. Breakfast was served from eight to nine."

"What?"

"We told everyone the time last night, and everyone else made it. Did you oversleep?" Molly didn't like how defensive he made her feel.

Jonathan brushed aside her words. "Well, I need breakfast now. My blood sugar will get too low if I don't have food. Make me an egg white omelet with cheese and tomatoes, toast, and coffee. I'll be in the den."

Molly surveyed the man with his pout and his aggressive stance. He was so unpleasant. Somehow the blue chamois shirt and the stiff new jeans were wrong on him. He was a man for designer labels. Back in California, everyone undoubtedly jumped when he barked a command because he had power. Well, he didn't have power here, and he didn't have power over her.

"Please do not speak to me that way." She tried to keep her voice neutral but was afraid her dislike leaked through.

He blinked in astonishment and his face grew red. His hands went to his hips. "What did you say?"

His soft tone of leashed displeasure chilled her. She couldn't imagine how it affected people whose livelihoods depended on his good favor. She, however, could stand up for herself.

"I'm not used to being spoken to so rudely, Jonathan. I am not your servant."

He glared at her while she stared calmly back. At the bakehouse, she would rush to the kitchen for a customer request. But something about him made her doubt he had blood sugar problems. Entitlement and hunger seemed to be his main ailments.

She gave him a sweet smile, knowing it would aggravate him. "There might still be some juice or coffee cake on the coffee bar in the den. You are welcome to check. And it won't be too long until lunch. I'll be on my way to the kitchen to start working on it soon."

"I hate this place." He glared at her as if she were personally responsible for his unhappiness. "If Rocky and Adrian move here . . ." He shook his head. "I might as well kill myself now."

Molly thought he was overreacting, but she didn't point it out. "Try to imagine the view out to the lake in better weather. The beautiful golf course. The sparkling water. Even the sand traps have a certain charm."

He snorted. "Second-rate golf courses can't make up for incompetence and stupid choices."

Second-rate? She narrowed her eyes, offended on Fergus's behalf. Major competitions were held here, televised worldwide. Celebrities chose to stay in the elegant resort to rest and recuperate, and important businesspeople held international conferences here. Jonathan was obviously too self-absorbed to see a beautiful thing right in front of him.

What she really wanted to do was to question him about where he'd been when the most recent shot was fired. Instead she asked, "With all the modern methods of communication available, why would Rocky living here be so bad?"

"In this business the answer is obvious," Jonathan growled.

"Out of sight, out of mind. They'll become obsolete. No one will think of them for roles." His expression took on a savage ferocity that unnerved Molly deep in her bones. "Believe me, if Rocky and Adrian move here, there won't be time for their careers to die. I'll kill them myself!"

13

Molly stared. Had she heard him correctly? And did he mean he'd kill the careers or the men?

There was a beat of absolute silence as Jonathan apparently heard himself. Voicing threats to men or careers was unwise in any situation, whether they were serious or not. When there was a trigger-happy gunman on the premises shooting at the man in question, it was not merely wrong—it was plain stupid.

With a flash of insight, Molly knew that comment showed the depth of Jonathan's fear as well as his anger at things he couldn't control. Maybe it also showed a genuine desire to harm—she'd have to mull that over some more—but it definitely indicated that he was terrified about his own future if the Sinclairs moved here. He was afraid of the loss of income and the loss of prestige. The haughty and condescending Jonathan Hooper was afraid. Who'd have thought?

His cheeks faded from angry red to embarrassed pink. "Um, I didn't mean . . ."

Molly gave an insincere smile. "Of course not."

"It's something you say when you're frustrated."

Or very, very angry. Jonathan could apologize all day, but she'd heard the fury in his voice. Enough to try to kill his golden goose? Or maybe just enough to frighten the Sinclairs back to the safety of southern California? Had he fired the shots as a misguided effort to get his clients to see things his way? Was it merely bad luck that

Adam had zigged when he should have zagged? Perhaps murder wasn't the goal after all. Perhaps.

Molly thought back to the two shootings and found herself wondering about Jonathan's whereabouts. He hadn't been in the gym earlier that morning, so where had he been? Hiding in the locker room hallway waiting for his chance to deliberately miss his most lucrative client?

Jonathan gave what he undoubtedly thought was an ingratiating smile, but it came off completely phony. "You don't have to tell the lady cop what I said, do you? The last thing I want is her on my back. I mean, I wasn't really threatening Rocky or Adrian. They're my friends as well as my clients."

The agent's white hair gleamed in the hallway light. His chamois shirt and jeans were crisp, and his tanned skin smooth. The only thing slightly wrinkled was his ego.

"Of course." She started for Chet's office, realizing she'd never gotten Bobby that pain reliever he'd requested.

"Of course what?" Jonathan called. "Of course yes, you're going to report? Or of course no, you're not?"

Molly didn't dignify his questions with an answer. Instead, she quickly retrieved Bobby's painkiller and gave it to him in the den. Leaving a content Angus snoozing by the fire, she went up to her room to grab clothes and toiletries for a quick shower in the gym. Once she was clean, she made her way to the kitchen to see what Laura wanted her to do for lunch prep.

In the kitchen, she found Adrian emerging from a kitchen closet with a can of white beans in one hand and tomato puree in the other.

"I'm making vegetable soup." He gestured toward the storm. "If ever a day called for soup, it's today."

"Sounds wonderful. Can I help?"

"Sure. Will you cut up carrots, onion, and green beans? I'll get the base going and parboil the potatoes."

Paula walked in, uncertainty written on her pretty features. "Do you want my help too?"

Laura smiled at Paula in her flannel shirt and jeans, an amusing match for the turquoise boots she still wore. "We're going to make grilled cheese sandwiches. Why don't you butter the bread?"

"O-okay." Paula collected butter, bread, and a knife, and began. It took several slices of bread torn to shreds before she got the hang of it. "I'm so sorry," she told Laura, tears brimming in her eyes. "I've made a mess."

"Don't worry about the bread," Laura said soothingly, whisking the abused slices away. "We'll make croutons out of them for the salad at dinner."

"You can do that?" Paula sounded amazed.

"A good kitchen uses everything," Laura said.

"How's it coming?" Adrian came to Molly's side and inspected her pile of chopped onion. "Any tears?"

"A few," Molly said with a chuckle.

"Comes with the territory." He grabbed a knife and began chopping the potatoes he'd parboiled in the microwave.

"Can I ask you a question, Adrian?" Molly asked, trying to keep her tone casual as she began peeling carrots. He was wearing a blue-and-green plaid flannel shirt and, unlike Jonathan, seemed at ease in the casual wear.

"Sure. Ask away. I might even have an answer." He grinned and winked at her.

Molly cleared her throat, knowing the question was deeply personal. "Why do you and Rocky stay with Jonathan Hooper?"

Adrian laughed. "He is a pain, isn't he? He used to be such a good guy. He took a huge chance on me when I was new on the scene.

It paid off for both of us. When Rocky decided to become an actor, I sent him to Jonathan. Again, they both benefitted from the arrangement."

"But he's . . ." Molly didn't know how to continue.

"He's all that and more," Adrian agreed. "Succeeding as one of Hollywood's premier agents has made him a failure as a human."

"So he really is a big-time wheeler-dealer?"

"He is, and he'll be happy to tell you so."

"If you guys move up here, he'll still represent you, won't he?" Molly glanced at Adrian for confirmation.

Adrian nodded. "But I think he's scared."

"I thought the same thing," Molly said. "If he would get off his high horse and actually listen to Rocky's concerns, things would be better."

"They would, but he's got real worries at the agency." Adrian continued chopping. "He recently took on a couple of new clients who were supposed to be the next big things. He landed them great roles and contracts, lots of money, and they bombed. Big-time. The studios lost cash and Jonathan lost face. His reputation took a big hit, to say nothing of his bank account."

"So he's afraid that if you move here, he'll lose the income from representing the two of you," Molly surmised. "Another big hit."

"That's my take," Adrian agreed. "He's forgetting that despite living in Beverly Hills, we still have to go on location for pretty much every film. Nothing would change there except the airport we fly out of."

While the soup simmered on the stove, Laura made chocolate chip cookies and Carol took over the sandwiches, to Paula's obvious relief.

Carol patted her hand. "There are little bags of potato chips and pretzels in the pantry. Grab a good mix, then find a big container to put the choices in."

"Then take them to the serving table," Paula finished, seemingly bolstered by being given a task she could do easily.

Molly shifted her attention to the practicalities of serving lunch. She made sure there were plates, soup bowls, and silver on the buffet table as well as napkins and condiments. She checked the coffee bar, brewed fresh coffee, and put out a selection of chilled soft drinks beside a bowl of ice.

Just before it was time to eat, Paula brought a large basket bearing an artistic arrangement of bagged chips and pretzels. Carol carried out the grilled cheese sandwiches, some plain, some with tomatoes, some with ham. Laura presented a tray of fresh cookies as well as one with the remaining goodies from the bakery. Adrian muscled his pot of soup to the table and assumed a position behind it, ladle in hand.

When the buffet tables were arranged to Molly's satisfaction, she took a step backward to take in the full effect and make sure she hadn't missed anything. She bumped into a solid figure at the same time she trod on a foot.

"Oof!"

Molly found Bobby behind her. "I'm so sorry," she said. "I didn't realize you were there."

"No problem." Bobby's forehead sported a large bruise, and he had the beginnings of two black eyes. "Is there time for me to go to the locker room to change out of my workout gear?"

Molly smiled at him. "Certainly. There's plenty of food."

Moving like an old man with creaky joints, Bobby trudged toward the gym. He paused before entering the room. "Are you sure it's safe to go in there?"

"Greer and I searched the men's locker room thoroughly. No one's hiding there."

Bobby lifted his chin, squared his shoulders, and continued on. Five minutes later, he returned, still moving stiffly but wearing khakis and a bright-blue sweater. He went to the end of the line, and by the time he went into the den to sit and eat, he was almost smiling.

After everyone had gone through the line, Molly helped herself. When she stepped into the den, Fergus waved to her. He'd saved her a seat.

"Great soup, Adrian." Jonathan spoke as if surprised.

"I've been telling you for years that I cook." Adrian shook his head. "Maybe now you'll believe me."

Jonathan made a noncommittal noise.

Adrian gave a wounded sniff. "You'll believe when I start my food company, Sinclair's Best."

"Yes, that would convince me," Jonathan said drily.

"Uncle Adrian's a great cook," Trace put in, spooning up soup at the time-honored speed of growing teenage boys the world over. Hero sat beside the boy's chair and watched every bite he took.

"We are not feeding the dog at the table, Trace." Rocky's voice was firm.

Trace frowned. "I'm not feeding him. People food isn't good for dogs."

"Hero, go lie down." Rocky pointed to the fireplace, where Angus was napping. Hero apparently saw that Angus had no food and stayed where he was, ever hopeful.

Molly suppressed a laugh when Trace turned to listen to something his uncle was saying and Rocky pulled a chunk of the ham from his sandwich and dropped it. She didn't think it even hit the floor before the dog vacuumed it up neatly.

People lingered at the table, enjoying the cookies and the conversation. When they began to stand, Greer and Rocky approached Fergus.

"Fergus, can I speak with you?" she asked.

"Sure." Fergus gestured. "Have a seat."

Bobby had risen, but remained where he was when he saw Greer and Rocky sit down across from Fergus.

Greer shot Molly a silent plea. Understanding, Molly stood and approached Bobby. Greer was asking Fergus about searching the basement, but Bobby didn't need to know that.

"How did you like lunch, Bobby?" Molly angled herself so that Bobby had to put his back to the table to speak with her. "Did it help with your headache?"

Bobby shrugged. "I enjoyed the food." He patted his middle. "As always. But I think it was the painkillers that did the most."

Molly noted that Greer was still talking to Fergus, so she gestured toward the window. "Can you believe this storm?" She walked toward the window. Social etiquette required the real estate agent to go with her, and he reluctantly did so.

Outside, the wind howled and the snow swirled. It was Mother Nature at her ferocious best—or worst, depending on how you looked at it.

Bobby sighed. "I keep thinking of my poor car out there getting buried. It'll take forever to dig it out."

"Spring's bound to come eventually. The snow will melt then."

"An eternal optimist, are you?"

"Glass half full, that's me. You know, this is the protected side of the building," Molly said. "Let's go see what it's like on the other side where the wind is whipping off the lake." She patted the side of her leg and called, "Come on, Angus."

The Scottie, also a glass-half-full individual, scampered toward her with his tail wagging. With a last baleful glance toward Greer, who was still talking to Fergus with Rocky at her side, Bobby followed as well.

In the gym, they gazed through the windows out to a vista of madness. The snow blew sideways under the power of the screaming wind. Several inches had been added to the snowpack since the previous day. The sky was invisible through the dense whiteout.

"Imagine what would have happened to Hero if Trace hadn't seen him." Molly shivered at the idea of the dog still being out there. She laid a fingertip on the glass and found it cold to the touch. "I'm so glad Fergus invited us to stay here. Otherwise Angus and I would be huddled under blankets in my apartment, probably with no electricity or heat."

"Me too, but at least I've got a fireplace," Bobby said. "I'd put my sleeping bag on the hearth and be toasty, at least until I had to eat."

"I suppose I could do the same by the bakehouse fireplace," Molly mused. "But this is less lonely and more fun."

"If you want to call it that." Bobby stepped so close to the windows he could have rested his nose against the glass if he leaned forward an inch. He stiffened with a shout. "There's a body in the hot tub!"

14

"A body?" Molly felt a chill that had nothing to do with the weather. She mentally ran through the list of people enjoying Fergus's hospitality. They'd all been at lunch, hadn't they? Had the shooter actually killed someone?

She stepped close to the glass and followed Bobby's shaking finger. Through the screen of snow, she could make out a form floating on its back in the steaming hot tub. The tub's lid lay on an angle, leaning against the tub's side.

"See? A body!" Bobby ran toward the den, calling for Greer.

Molly narrowed her eyes as she peered through the glass. The body moved, and her heart jumped. The bottom half of the body disappeared into the water. The upper half lowered itself until all but the head was underwater. *That's no dead body.*

Hero appeared and sat beside Angus. Molly couldn't believe Trace had let the dog get more than five feet from him, then realized that the dog watched the scene outdoors with an air of longing. She studied the body in the hot tub, which now had snow gathering on its hair.

Greer dashed into the gym with Bobby scrambling behind her. ". . . just lying there," he was saying.

"Face up or down?" Greer put her hand to the window.

Bobby frowned, confused. "Um, I don't know. Molly?"

"Neither," Molly replied. "It's Trace, and he's sitting. Perfectly alive."

Rocky strolled in. "I would have told you if you hadn't run off so fast." He smiled at Greer.

"You knew about this?" the officer asked.

Rocky shrugged. "He wanted to get in the hot tub in the snow so badly. You heard him talk about it last evening. Adrian and I decided why not."

"I'll tell you why not." Bobby sounded more than a little miffed. "You scare people to death."

"We never meant for anything like that to happen," Rocky assured him. "We were trying to grant the kid's wish. This move is distressing to him, taking him from the only life he's known. He was so young, less than a year old, when our parents died. He doesn't remember them, which is a shame because they were so excited about him. Talk about a surprise." He adopted his movie star grin. "I was twenty when he was born."

Bobby relaxed a little. Molly thought it was the poor-orphaned-Trace bit that eased his anger. How could he justify being mad at the poor kid?

Rocky stuck his hands in his jeans pockets. "Having a brother instead of a mother and father hasn't been easy for him, especially when he's stuck with nannies when I'm on location. Adrian helps as much as he can, but it's still difficult."

Greer stared at Rocky in fascination, and Molly could see her preconceived notions of the action star crumbling further under the weight of his sincere concern for his little brother. He'd taken on the responsibility of raising Trace at the young age of twenty, which would be hard for anyone.

Fergus joined the cluster by the window. "Trace asked me to turn off the alarm so he could sit in the tub in the snow. For some reason, he thinks it'll be fun." He shrugged. "He's thirteen."

Bobby stared at the boy, who was now sinking completely under the surface and then popping back up over and over. "I still say he's crazy."

"Nobody's arguing that point," Rocky said.

"He's out there alone." Greer ran a hand through her hair as she gazed out at the boy. "That's so dangerous."

"Don't worry," Rocky said. "Adrian's standing guard at the door to make sure he's okay."

Greer visibly relaxed at that news.

Rocky watched his brother. "Yesterday you'd have thought we were the vilest of villains when we asked him to help with the ditch. 'It's too cold. It's too wet.'" His voice sounded remarkably like Trace's. "And now he goes out in this storm for fun."

Fergus bumped Rocky with his elbow. "We'd better get our coats. He'll be a prune soon. Time to put the lid back on the tub."

"You're going out in this?" Bobby swept a hand toward the window and the storm beyond.

"For a couple of minutes. That's all it'll take. And we've got the proper weather gear now, thanks to Molly." Rocky grinned at her.

Bobby opened his mouth as if he wanted to say more, but the Sinclairs were potential clients, so he pressed his lips together and took a deep breath. "I can help too," he said, sounding anything but willing. "I'll get my coat."

Fergus held up a hand. "You're a wounded warrior, Bobby. Thanks, but no thanks."

Bobby touched the bump on his head and tried to appear disappointed. "Okay. If you say so."

When Fergus and Rocky left, Greer started for the den. "I need to get my bag. I left it behind in my hurry to get here."

"I'll come with you." Bobby hurried after her.

Molly decided she wanted to see Trace when he came back inside. She thought she knew which door Adrian was guarding, where Rocky and Fergus would exit. She headed in that direction with Angus and

Hero at her heels. Sure enough, she found Adrian in the hall behind the locker rooms.

Adrian held the outside door open a crack, clutching the edge so the wind didn't rip it from his grasp. He glanced at Molly as she stepped into the hall. "Is there an Upper Peninsula cure for frostbitten fingers?"

Molly grew instantly concerned. "Are you serious?"

His answer was a wide grin. "The kid's having a ball, but I'm about frozen. And we still have to put the lid back on the hot tub."

Rocky walked out of the locker room clad in his winter clothes in time to hear his uncle's comments. He patted him on the back. "You did your duty and more. Fergus and I will take care of the lid."

Adrian didn't argue.

"Want to help?" Fergus teased Molly as he pulled his knit cap down over his ears.

Rocky tucked his pant legs into his boots. "You can lift one corner of the lid."

Molly held up her hands. "That doesn't even deserve an answer."

Adrian stepped back from the door, and Fergus and Rocky pushed through and into the storm. The door slammed shut behind them. Molly hugged herself, glad for the teal fleece she had on over her knit top. She and the dogs did their best to ignore the icy blast that threaded through the hall.

Trace came running in wearing his swimsuit and snow boots. Goose bumps stood out all over his skin. He quickly wrapped himself in the towel Adrian handed him. He jogged in place in an effort to get warm, wearing a huge grin. "So cool."

"Did you get pictures?" Molly asked. "Your friends in sunny California will want proof."

"Uncle Adrian took some when I first got in. Then he wimped out and came inside."

Adrian put his nose in the air, though Molly didn't miss the twinkle in his eye. "I'm not stupid enough to stand there and freeze."

Hero braced his front paws on Trace's thighs, and Trace bent and rubbed his ears. "That was so great. You'd have loved it, boy."

"I doubt that," Adrian muttered.

"Wasn't it cold?" Molly asked the trembling boy.

"On my head, but the water was nice and hot," Trace said. "Mr. MacGregor heated it for me."

Adrian tousled his nephew's hair. "All for you, kid. All for you. If I get pneumonia, I expect you to take care of me."

"Deal." Trace pulled open the door to the locker room. "I'm freezing. Time for a hot shower."

The door to the outside flew open again, and Fergus and Rocky rushed in, brushing snow off their clothes and stamping their feet.

"That was great of you, guys." Molly smiled at all three men. "Trace is one happy kid."

Rocky gave a satisfied grin. "Since we can't or won't always do what he wants, it's nice when we can give him something he has his heart set on." He and Adrian disappeared into the locker room.

Fergus pulled off his cap and turned to Molly. "Greer wants to search the basement."

"I know."

"I'm going with her."

Molly grabbed his hand. "And I want to go with you."

"Why am I not surprised?" Fergus smiled. He understood her so well.

Ten minutes later, the dogs were in the den and Molly stood with Greer, Fergus, and Rocky at the top of a flight of concrete steps that wound down into darkness.

Fergus flipped a switch that lighted the stairwell. "Down there are the guts of the place. Maintenance, laundry, storage, disposal, electrical room."

"I'll give the area a quick search," Greer said. "You guys wait here. If I shout, call for backup."

Rocky frowned. "Greer, I was just outside. There is no way backup is coming, no matter how great the need."

Greer made a face. "I know. That was stupid to say, but I can't let you go down there until I get the lay of the land. I can't take a chance you'll be harmed."

"You're not 'letting' me do anything." Rocky was in full Matt Bryant mode. "I'm choosing to go down there whether you like it or not." He indicated Molly and Fergus. "We're your backup."

Greer glared, likely both irritated at Rocky and uncertain about letting any of them go into possible danger. Going down alone was foolish, but there was a would-be murderer somewhere in the building, and they needed as many sets of eyes looking for him as they could get.

"Don't worry." Fergus started down the steps, Molly right behind him. "He'll hear us. Stealth is not our strong suit. Or he'll see us when the lights come on. He won't hang around to see what we want."

Greer gave an exasperated growl, then followed Fergus and Molly with Rocky beside her.

The growl of the generator, vented to the outside with great conduits, got louder and louder as they descended, easily overwhelming the crackle and buzz of the fluorescent lights overhead. At the bottom of the stairs, Fergus hit another switch. A vast area yawned before them. Molly stared at the enormous pieces of equipment filling the space, everything from industrial-size washing machines and dryers to giant tool benches with every conceivable tool, from heating and air conditioning equipment with their massive vents to massive refuse bins on wheels.

A room with a sign that bore the word *DANGER* and a lightning bolt housed the electrical system, humming with the responsibility of keeping the one working wing alive.

Fergus raised his voice to be heard over the generator's roar. "Don't go in there. It's too dangerous." He tried the knob, but it didn't budge. He nodded in satisfaction and indicated the number pad that controlled access. "Still locked. Our man isn't in there and hasn't been."

Molly surveyed the vast space and found its size and shadows unnerving. When staff was here, walking around, doing their jobs, talking without the generator as competition, everything would be fine. But now the corners were bathed in a murky gloom, and her imagination had someone hiding behind one of the big machines, or behind one of the support pillars, or in one of the storage closets.

"How do you want to work this, Greer?" Fergus asked.

Greer stood with her hands on her hips. "We've got to remember he's dangerous and has a gun."

Molly swallowed at the reminder. The threatening shadows suddenly felt deeper and darker.

"I think Fergus is probably right," Greer continued. "It's likely that we've already scared him off, but we can't know that for certain."

Rocky leaned forward, eagerness in every line of his body. "Give us our assignments so we can get to it."

"This isn't one of your movies, Rocky," Greer said. "You're not Matt Bryant."

"And you aren't the damsel in distress Matt's supposed to rescue," Rocky countered. "You are a very capable cop. But I'm here to help, and I intend to."

Greer seemed to analyze him before a slight smile crossed her lips. "You're not as bad as I thought you'd be, cowboy."

Rocky gave her a steely stare, but there was a twinkle in his eyes. "And don't you forget it."

If Molly wasn't mistaken, Greer's cheeks pinked slightly before she clapped her hands, getting back to business. "Fergus, you and Molly take the right side. Rocky and I will take the left. Open every door. Search each room and closet for any sign of him. Check behind all machinery. But be careful. Please."

Molly had every intention of being exactly that. While she headed toward the laundry, Fergus went to check around the generator. The decibel level was almost painful, and she couldn't help but wonder what it would be like without the sound suppression insulation.

She started her search with a row of four massive dryers. She didn't think anyone could hide behind them since they were up against a wall, but she checked anyway. She even opened the doors and looked in the tumblers. The machines were large enough that a person could hide inside—though if they did so, there would be no chance of escape if you were discovered.

Neat piles of folded towels, blankets, and bed runners were piled on counters, and large flat iron machines stood silent sentry awaiting the next workday when they'd help iron and fold sheets, tablecloths, and napkins. A large, freestanding closet at least ten feet long stood nearby with doors on the two long sides. Those working in the laundry could put their finished work in from one side, and the supply personnel could come to the other, more easily accessible side to pull out the linens to distribute to the maids and dining rooms upstairs.

The big closet was as neat and organized as it was supposed to be. Piles of clean, pressed linens waited for the next shift to grab what they needed. There were scores of extra pillows and a stack of uniforms. All was in perfect order—except for a slightly askew pile of quilts.

The last person to pull a quilt free had left the now top one twisted. Molly resisted the impulse to straighten it and instead shut the door.

She moved on to a regular closet that read *Janitorial Supplies* on the door. She pulled open the door and gave a shriek. "Greer, Fergus! Come quick!"

15

"You found him?" Greer sprinted across the huge room, Rocky beside her.

Molly made a face, regretting how excitedly she'd sounded the alarm. "Sorry. No."

Fergus reached her first and took hold of her arms, examining her with concern. "Are you okay? You scared me."

Even with the stress of the situation, a warm feeling swept through her. "I'm fine. Really, I am."

"If you say so." He gave her a quick hug anyway.

Greer moved around Molly and peered into the supply closet. "Did you go in?"

"No." Molly gave a disbelieving huff. "Isn't it funny how you search for something, but you don't really expect to find it?"

The closet, like most closets of its sort, had its walls lined with shelves and an open area in the middle for people to move around. The shelves held jugs of cleaning fluids, boxes of replacement parts, squirt bottles, cloths—anything housekeeping might need. The corners were full of propped mops, brooms, and janitorial-size sweepers.

In the middle of the room on the floor was a nest of quilts identical to those in the big linen closet. Remembering the untidy stack, Molly could just see someone pulling a bunch of the quilts free, catching the corner of the next one down, and leaving it mussed.

Beside the quilts lay a pair of pillows.

"You can layer all the quilts you want, but the floor is still hard."

Fergus rubbed his lower back.

"He should have slept on a stack of pillows," Rocky said. "Still, it wouldn't be as nice as his comfy bed upstairs."

Molly agreed. "Talk about a downgrade. Though, come to think of it, he never got to sleep in his comfy bed upstairs, did he? We found him first."

"And we feel so sorry for him," Rocky murmured sarcastically.

Greer snapped photos of the makeshift bed. "Funny how you found his room upstairs, Molly, and you discovered this hidey-hole too."

"Too bad I can't actually find the man himself," Molly grumbled.

Greer grabbed the duffel that sat beside the quilts and unzipped it. "Not the gunman. The photographer. There are two cameras inside." She smiled at Rocky. "No more secret pictures."

Rocky shook his head as he assessed the bag's contents. "He's still got his long-lensed camera with him, wherever he is."

Greer zipped open a second duffel, revealing rumpled men's clothing. "Well, he won't have his clothes or personal belongings any longer. I'm confiscating these. We're slowly shrinking his world. We'll get him yet."

Fergus gathered the quilts, towels, and pillows and dumped them in the dirty laundry bin. Rocky slung one duffel over his shoulder. Greer carried the other.

"So he's still skulking around the resort. How creepy," Molly said. "You really don't think he's the shooter?"

"I don't believe he's the gunman, but he is definitely a creep," Greer said firmly.

"You're a black-and-white kind of girl, aren't you?" Rocky sounded intrigued.

Greer frowned. "Is there something wrong with that?"

"Not at all," Rocky said. "It'll be fun to argue the value of gray with you."

"Gray?" the officer repeated wryly. "What's that?"

Rocky grinned. "I can't wait."

Molly suppressed a smile at the obvious attraction between the pair.

Fergus took Molly's hand. "I think we'd better head upstairs."

Molly checked her watch. "It's time to get dinner going. I need to report to the kitchen."

Fergus rubbed a hand over his face and stifled a yawn. "I've got some work to do in my office."

"Did you get any sleep last night?" she asked.

He managed a weary grin. "Things are bound to calm down soon. I hope."

She gave his hand a squeeze. "It's got to stop snowing eventually."

"How long will it take to be dug out?" Rocky asked as they climbed the stairs. "I need to get to Adam as soon as I can. He's still barely stable, and he needs to be surrounded by people who care about him."

"It'll happen faster than you'd expect," Fergus said. "Crews will be on the roads as soon as possible if they're not out there already. I've got a guy under contract to clear the resort parking lot, and he'll show as soon as the snow stops."

Glad to leave the basement behind, Molly headed for the kitchen. Laura was already there, staring into the big refrigerator.

She spun when she heard Molly and announced, "Someone's been taking food."

"You're sure?" Though Molly wondered why she was surprised. Lou Duckworth was sneaking around the place as if he moved through walls. The gunman was no slouch either. "Who do you think it is? The shooter? The photographer?"

"Good question."

"My money's on the photographer," Molly said. "We've found his latest hiding spot in the basement. Greer took his cameras and clothes this time."

"So he can't take any more pictures, but he can still steal food."

"Rocky says he still has the long-lens camera, so who knows? It depends on how nervy he is."

"Well, we have to protect our food supply," Laura said grumpily as she washed her hands. "He hasn't been invited to the party."

Adrian strolled in. "What are we making for dinner?"

"Someone's been stealing food." Laura glared at the refrigerator as if it was at fault.

"Duckworth." Adrian clearly wasn't surprised. "The man's got nerve, I'll say that for him."

"Molly says they've found him," Laura reported.

Adrian's gaze snapped to Molly. "Where?"

"In the basement, but it wasn't him exactly," Molly corrected. "It was his stuff, except for the big camera."

"Poor Rocky," Adrian said.

Carol walked in. "Any thoughts for dinner?" she asked. "For dessert, I'm making us a chocolate cake with raspberry filling and buttercream icing. And I thought a crisp Caesar salad would be good with whatever you've got for dinner. There's lots of romaine in the crisper."

"I'm going to make my own version of ratatouille with the fresh vegetables we have," Adrian said. "If that's okay with you, Laura."

"Sounds wonderful. It'll go well with the baked chickens I'm prepping." Laura began rubbing salt and pepper on the birds.

"Is there cranberry sauce?" Molly asked as she pulled clean tablecloths from the supply station.

"Of course," Laura answered. "Can't have baked chicken without it."

Conversation was minimal during dinner as everyone enjoyed the delicious feast the Bakehouse Three and Adrian had prepared. Molly didn't want to ruin the moment by bringing up Lou Duckworth or the shooter, and she assumed nobody else wanted to break the spell either. But after plates were cleared and everyone was relaxing with their coffee or tea, conversation picked up. The tone was mostly genial—until Jonathan couldn't keep quiet any longer.

"Rocky, why on earth do you want to live in this wasteland?" He gestured toward the window, now a black wall beyond which wind still howled and snow still fell.

"Wait until the storm passes," Greer said. "It'll be beautiful. Cross-country skiing. Sledding. Snowman building."

Trace's bored expression brightened. "I've never gotten to build a snowman. Do you really put a carrot for the nose?"

"If you want to," Greer said. "And coal for eyes and mouth, if you can find any."

Jonathan harrumphed. "There's no rush building your snowman, Trace. This dump of slush is going to be here for months."

Rocky shrugged. "That's what winter up here means. Snow for months."

Jonathan's expression soured further. "And you'd pick this over warmth and sunshine year round?"

"Some things are more important than warm weather," Rocky said.

Jonathan glared at Rocky and took off on a new bent. "Think of all the opportunities you'll be denying Trace if you move up here. Culture like museums and theater. Fun like the beach and the ocean. The redwoods. Wine country."

Adrian raised an eyebrow. "The boy's thirteen, Jonathan. I don't think wine country is in his immediate future."

"I will miss the beach," Trace admitted. "And surfing."

Greer's eyes lit up. "There's wonderful surfing on the Great Lakes. Lake Superior has several good spots, and so does Lake Michigan. It's different than saltwater surfing and colder than California and Hawaii, but there are great waves."

"You sound like you know what you're talking about." Rocky studied her with ever-increasing interest.

"I do," Greer said. "Bring your wet suits, and I'll show you great surfing not far from here."

Rocky glanced at Trace, who remained looking skeptical.

"Oh, come on, Rocky." Jonathan's voice rose. "You're a smart man. Don't let a pretty lady turn your head. You don't want to kill your career."

"Enough, Jonathan." There was steel in Rocky's voice.

"I was talking to my father earlier." Paula finger combed her hair nervously. "I asked him what he thought of you moving up here."

"Paula, this is not your father's concern," Rocky said sternly.

"Yeah," she said, "but as head of a major studio, he knows everything about the business."

"He probably does, but we were trying to keep things quiet until after we were settled here," Rocky said. "Why would you talk about us with him?"

"I had to tell him about you to explain why I was coming to the UP," Paula answered. "But he won't spread the news. I mean, why would he tell? Who would he tell?"

"Anyone in the movie business for starters." Adrian shook his head at her naivete. "There are always ears listening and sources eager for news."

In spite of Rocky's attempt to keep his voice steady, his frustration leaked out. "Paula, I know you didn't mean to cause trouble—"

Her eyes went wide. "Never. And neither would my father."

Rocky wasn't convinced. "Your father can kill a career like that."

He snapped his fingers and Paula jumped. "I know he can dent mine badly, and I'm not one of his players. But if he did come down on me, my private life is not his business."

"But it is mine." Paula's voice was meek and apologetic, and her fingers flew through her hair. "My job depends on you."

"Your job depends on Sol, not me, and he knows I've done everything the studio asked and more. Just because he suddenly decided it wasn't enough . . ."

"That's this industry," Jonathan said. "We both know it's never enough. That's why you need to be near Hollywood."

"Jonathan, we both know plenty of actors do not live in Southern California," Rocky retorted.

"But they have their main homes there." Jonathan thumped his fist on the table. "The houses somewhere else are vacation homes, not primary residences. They go there for two weeks, a month tops."

Rocky stood, his posture all Matt Bryant ready to take on the world. "Jonathan, you will not say another word to me about this move."

"But—"

"Or I will find another agent." Rocky spoke each word slowly and distinctly. He leaned across the table until his nose was inches from Jonathan's. "Understood?" Then he stalked from the room.

A thundering silence buffeted the room following Rocky's departure. It was as if no one had the courage to speak. Molly met Laura's eyes across the table, and they grimaced at each other.

Finally, Adrian rose. "Jonathan, you of all people should know that negotiations should always be made from a position of strength, not panic." He waited for his words to sink in, eyes skewering Jonathan for what felt like a very long time, then turned to his nephew. "Trace, come on over here with Hero and help me find the last pieces of the puzzle I've been working on."

Trace rose quickly and followed Adrian, Hero tripping along at his side. With that movement, the group came to life again.

Harvey stood and began clearing away the dirty dishes. "Come help me wash up, Bobby, Chet, Trent." He didn't leave room for the men to beg off.

Trent rose immediately. "Only fair."

Bobby began clearing up with a vengeance as well. Chet happily displayed his muscles by carrying the full tubs of dishes off to the kitchen as if they weighed nothing.

Jonathan wandered casually to his chair by the fire, making a show of not being shaken by the anger and threat of one of his major clients. He sank into his seat and pulled out his phone. He became absorbed in something on it, though Molly wondered how much reception he actually had.

What struck her as interesting was that after a few minutes, Paula hesitantly took the chair next to him. She sat quietly for a minute while Jonathan ignored her. Then she took a deep breath and spoke to him in a low voice. At first, it was obvious that he couldn't care less what she wished to say to him and was barely listening. But as she soldiered on, a spark of interest lit in his eyes, and soon they were engaged in a serious discussion, though Paula fiddled with her hair the whole time.

"I'd love to be a fly on the wall for that conversation," Laura muttered in Molly's ear.

Molly raised an eyebrow at her. "You mean the Hollywood power broker and the Hollywood princess? Me too."

Carol came over, and the three women collapsed on one of the couches. "What are we doing for breakfast tomorrow, Laura?" Carol asked

"We can do pancakes, but we need protein too." Laura slipped off her shoes and put her stockinged feet on the coffee table. She crossed her ankles.

"Everyone likes bacon," Molly said.

"We need a healthy protein too," Laura said. "I'm thinking eggs of some kind."

"An egg casserole?" Carol suggested.

"Do we have to make it tonight?" Molly wasn't in favor of going back to the kitchen.

"I've got one we can whip up tomorrow morning." Laura glanced from Molly to Carol. "Now tell me, who do you think broke the window in the gym?"

"What do you mean?" Carol put her sock-clad feet on the coffee table too.

"I'm wondering why the photographer would break a window," Laura mused.

"You're right," Carol replied thoughtfully. "He had nothing to gain."

"And why would the shooter?" Laura continued.

Molly frowned. "Again, we've got no good reason." She was silent as the implications sank in. "You don't think we've got a third troublemaker running around, do you?"

"That's a bit absurd." Carol's tone was disbelieving.

"I know," Laura admitted. "But every time I think about all that's happened, none of the pieces fit together."

"They don't." Molly tucked one leg under herself. "They really don't," she repeated thoughtfully.

A shadow fell over her. Paula stood there, one hand wrapped around a mug, the other fiddling with her hair. "We're out of hot water and peppermint tea again."

Molly sat up straight. "How can that be?"

"I drink it when I'm nervous."

"I'll say you do." Molly rose. "Come with me. I'll show you where the tea and the water are so you can get your own in the future."

"Oh." Clearly Paula wasn't used to getting her own anything.

They walked out of the den together. Molly gazed sidelong at Paula, who was still nervously touching her hair. "You and Jonathan were having a good conversation, huh?"

"I had questions for him. I've been wondering if I'd like to be an agent. It's got to be better than jumping every time Sol shouts at me."

Molly screeched to a halt at the kitchen door and stared at Paula in astonishment. The girl didn't strike her as a good fit for a career that required a strong, decisive personality. "Why do you think you'd like that?"

"I know lots of young actors who are yearning for their big break," Paula answered. "If I was an agent, I could maybe help them get started."

"Are any of them talented at it, or are they only people you like?"

Paula's voice took on excitement. "I can tell the good from the bad, and these guys are good. I'm not as dumb as people think, you know. Naive maybe, and entitled. But I know talent. I'd love to help them."

Molly was impressed with the young woman's insight into herself. "But do you have the bulldog personality to push for your clients? Can you go toe-to-toe with the big guns for money or name placement or whatever else is important to your clients?"

Paula cringed. "I don't like confrontation."

Bobby came scurrying down the hall with a bundle of used dinner linens in his arms. He muttered something inarticulate and stepped around them into the kitchen area.

Molly shifted her attention back to Paula. "I think working as an agent means confrontation," she said. "Not necessarily angry confrontation, but holding to your position against powerful people and their pressure to fold and yield to their desires. Can you do that?"

Paula seemed unsure, a bad sign in Molly's estimation. "I just want to help people. Agents help people."

"They help one group of people by standing up to another." When Paula's shoulders slumped, Molly asked gently, "Do you really want my advice?"

"Yes." The young woman turned around, innocent eyes on Molly.

"I think you're too sweet for the hard-nosed business of being an agent," Molly said. "You don't want to spend your life arguing with people, do you?"

"No, you're right." Paula sighed deeply. "There's got to be some way I can help people. I'll figure it out someday."

Molly was about to offer more guidance about listening to her heart and taking into account what she was good at and enjoyed doing. But an alarming odor wafting toward her nose stopped her in her tracks. She grabbed Paula's arm. "Something's burning!"

Paula sniffed the air. "It's coming from the gym!"

They rushed down the hall and into the gym, hitting the light switch just inside the door. Everything appeared fine.

"There!" Paula cried, pointing, and Molly saw a haze of smoke coming from the direction of Chet's office and the locker rooms.

"Get help, Paula." Molly rushed across the gym and into the locker room hallway. Smoke edged out from under Chet's closed office door. Molly reached for the handle.

"No!" Paula knocked her hand aside.

Molly blinked, partly because she hadn't realized Paula was still with her and partly because she'd never seen Paula act so decisively.

"You always feel a door before you open it." Paula ran her hands over the wood. "If it's hot, it's too dangerous to open. The fire's too strong on the other side."

Molly put her hand to the door too. "It's cool."

Paula gripped the handle and pushed the door open.

A fire burned in a metal trash can sitting on top of Chet's desk, producing thick, acrid smoke. As Molly registered this, Paula lunged forward and blasted the flames with the contents of a bright-red fire extinguisher.

Molly looked from the foaming mess to Paula with shock and admiration. "You put it out."

Paula put the fire extinguisher on Chet's desk with a *thunk*, then coughed from the rank stench.

"Where'd you get the extinguisher?" Molly asked.

"In the gym." Paula waved vaguely. "I grabbed it as I ran through. I always notice where fire extinguishers are."

"Really?" Molly knew where they all were at Bread on Arrival, but they rarely stood out to her anywhere else.

Paula shrugged. "It's a silly little habit."

"Are you kidding? It's a wonderful habit. If that had burned much longer, it would have set off the sprinkler system. Can you imagine the damage?"

"What in the world?" Chet stood in the doorway. He advanced on the wastebasket as if it were a vicious enemy. He glanced from it to the ceiling. "Placed right under a sprinkler head. If you hadn't—" He narrowed his eyes suspiciously. "How did you know?"

"We smelled smoke." Molly gestured to Paula and the extinguisher. "She saved the day."

"Really?" Chet eyed Paula, who blushed. He appeared as surprised as Molly felt. "Well, thanks."

"Sure," Paula murmured.

Chet pulled out his phone and tapped at the screen. "I'm texting Fergus."

"I think I'll go back to the den." Paula began edging out of the room.

Before she made her escape through the gym, Fergus came running with Greer, Adrian, and Trace right behind him. Carol and Laura trailed them a bit more cautiously. Bringing up the rear was the kitchen cleanup crew of Harvey, Trent, and Bobby, the latter wiping soap suds off his hands as he came.

"We saw everyone run past. What's going on?" Harvey moved to Carol's side.

Angus and Hero pushed their way to the front of the crowd and sniffed the air with interest. They sneezed, the stench of smoke irritating their sensitive noses.

The only ones missing were Jonathan and Rocky.

The potential for destruction struck Fergus right away. He closed his eyes and shook his head. "Is it me?"

It was a whisper, but Molly heard him. She laid a comforting hand on his shoulder.

Greer snapped evidence pictures and declared Chet's office a crime scene.

Chet's mouth fell open. "You mean I can't use it?"

"I tell you what," Fergus said. "Why don't we lock the wastebasket in my office where it will be safe for you, Greer. Then Chet can use his office as he needs to. Nothing else was hurt, so that should be okay, right?"

Greer thought it over, then nodded. "Good compromise." She picked up the basket with gloved hands and started from the room. "I'll put this in your office, watch you lock it in, then go find Rocky to be sure he's safe."

"I'm here, and I'm fine." Rocky spoke from the back of the crowd. "I was on the way back to the den when I saw you all rush in here." He cleared his throat. "I owe everyone an apology for my little temper tantrum. I should have handled that more privately and professionally, rather than making you all uncomfortable with a public outburst like that."

"Don't let it worry you, Rocky." Adrian moved to his nephew's side. "You were not the one at fault. Jonathan has been pushing and pushing. I'm surprised you didn't explode sooner."

There were general murmurs of agreement. Molly caught Rocky eyeing Greer, seeking her forgiveness specifically. *How interesting.*

Greer gave him a cheeky smile. "Someone needed to give him as good as he gave. You did a fine job—strong, but polite. You should be a cop."

Everyone laughed while Rocky seemed much relieved. "By the way," he said, "I called the hospital. Adam has regained consciousness, but he's still very weak. It's a step in the right direction, though."

"He's a strong guy." Adrian clapped a hand on Rocky's shoulder. "If anyone can survive a wound like that, it's him."

Trace's face reflected his worry. "From your lips to God's ears, Uncle Adrian."

Hear, hear. Molly sent another of the many prayers she'd said since they had become snowbound. *We're counting on You, Lord.*

"Back to the den, everyone." Fergus held out his arms as if herding a clowder of cats. "Or off to bed. Whichever you prefer."

Laura nudged Molly and asked, "Den or upstairs?"

Before Molly could answer, Paula tapped her hesitantly on the arm. "My tea?"

"Right." In the excitement, she'd forgotten about what had brought them there in the first place. Well, if anyone deserved her tea, it was Paula. "Come on. Laura, do you want something hot to drink? I think it'll help soothe our nerves."

"A cup of decaf sounds nice," Laura said.

Everyone trailed back into the den, grabbing drinks and second desserts and settling to conversations or projects. Adrian and Trace went back to their jigsaw puzzle with Rocky and Greer peering over their shoulders, and occasionally reaching in to add pieces. Paula sat by Chet and Bobby, who finally realized he had a beautiful woman beside him and stopped casting woeful puppy-dog eyes at Greer. Carol and Harvey grabbed cups of tea and disappeared upstairs. Trent settled beside Laura, and Fergus dropped onto the sofa beside Molly. Angus sprawled by the fire with Hero, his near constant companion these days.

While conversation and laughter buzzed about the room, Jonathan sat as though glued to his chair by the fire. He spoke to no one, and no one spoke to him. He didn't ask what the excitement had been about.

"That fire was a close one," Fergus said, exhaustion dripping from every word.

Molly gave him a sympathetic pat on the knee. "Are you okay?"

"I am. But I'm going to have nightmares for a long time about the sprinklers going off and ruining everything in this wing—computers, wooden gym floor, conference rooms, ballroom decor." He shuddered at the thought.

"Is that what would have happened?" Molly asked.

"No, only the one above the fire would have been activated, but it would have damaged Chet's computer and anything in the office. That would have been bad enough."

"You ought to give Paula a lifetime free pass to Castleglen."

"My thoughts exactly." Fergus smiled at the woman sitting with Chet and Bobby, talking easily with them, making even Bobby laugh. "She is such an enigma. I think she has more random pieces than that puzzle Adrian and Trace are working on."

Molly peeked at the Sinclairs. "I don't think Trace is working too hard."

The kid had his phone out and was holding it at various heights. Suddenly, his eyes lit up and he let out a whoop of excitement. "I've got reception," he announced. "And look what I found. You're going to love it, Greer."

"Another one? You're kidding." Rocky grabbed the phone and stared. Greer scowled. "When? How?"

"That's the basement," Rocky said. "It was taken when we were down there this afternoon."

Molly and Fergus peered over Rocky's shoulders to study the photo. Rocky and Greer were staring at each other, eyes bright, lips smiling, the chemistry obvious.

"He was at the far end of the basement, just watching us," Fergus said.

"Yuck." Molly rubbed her arms to warm away the chill.

"There's another set of stairs there," Fergus explained. "They're hardly ever used because the big service elevators are available. He must have been hanging there, ready to rush up the steps if we came that far."

"And we didn't." Disgust dripped from Greer's words. "After finding his stuff in the supply closet, we came back up the way we'd gone down. How could I have been so incompetent?"

Rocky rested a hand on her arm. "We were all there with you, Greer, so we're all to blame. And you are far from incompetent."

Greer's expression indicated that she remained unconvinced.

Rocky studied the picture and smiled. "Lovely." He held the phone out to her.

She gave Rocky a withering glare and stalked to the coffee bar. He grinned after her. She gave a quick glance over her shoulder and caught him. Her cheeks reddened, and he laughed.

Adrian winked at Trace, who beamed.

Molly and Fergus returned to their seats. He stretched his legs out, and she settled into his side with his arm around her shoulders.

Across the room, Chet jumped to his feet. He unzipped his Castleglen hoodie and tossed it on his chair. "Come on." He waved at Bobby and Paula. "Up you get."

Both shook their heads, but Chet didn't give up, and soon Bobby and Paula stood facing the wall, their hands stretched in front of them.

"Hands on the wall." Chet demonstrated. "Lean in and push back. Lean and push. Come on. It's a good way to work your upper body without weights if you're not used to doing strength training."

Molly had to smile at Bobby trying to move with the ease of the very fit trainer. "What's Chet's story?" she murmured to Fergus.

"About a year ago, I was searching for an activities manager to oversee the gym and the pools and other activities depending on the season. Someone told me about Chet."

"He already lived in Loch Mallaig?"

"He moved here with the idea of opening a gym. He had a pretty good business plan, but when I approached him, he decided he liked the idea of a guaranteed paycheck and a good health plan more than being an independent business owner."

Chet clapped Bobby on the back to encourage him while Bobby scrunched up his face unhappily.

"The guy is great at his job," Fergus said. "He's got several people who work under him, and they all like him. He's organized, goes the extra mile, and is always on the lookout for new programs we might add. I'm glad I found him." He squeezed her to his side. "But not as glad as I am that I found you."

Joy filled her. "Me too. Believe me."

"Mmm." He lay his head on the back of the seat and closed his eyes. In seconds, he was fast asleep. Molly smiled. It had been romantic for a second or two there.

Laura approached, Trent beside her. "I'm ready to go up." She smothered a yawn.

"I'm going up too," Trent said. "I'll walk you two to your door."

Molly leaned over and kissed Fergus on the cheek. "Good night," she whispered, then untangled herself from his arm and gathered Angus.

"Sleep tight," Paula called. She pulled a pair of blankets from a closet and started to make her bed on one of the couches. "I'm spending the night here again."

Molly waved as she followed Trent and Laura to the door. Chet and Bobby trailed them down the hall, across the lobby and up the dark stairwell. The upstairs hall was definitely colder than the previous night. Once inside her room, Molly thought the bedroom was colder still, especially with the wind beating against the window.

She closed the drapes. "We should have pulled these when we left this morning. It might not be so chilly."

"We'll do it tomorrow," Laura said as she retrieved pajamas from her bag.

They quickly got changed and brushed their teeth, and both women put on their spa robes over their nightclothes before climbing into bed.

"Come here, Angus." Laura patted the mattress beside her. "Get your warm little body up here to act as a heating pad."

Angus eagerly climbed under the covers and burrowed against Laura. In no time, he was snuffling contentedly in his sleep. Laura put her back against him for warmth and was soon fast asleep.

Molly surveyed the two sleeping forms and wished her thoughts would stop swirling in her mind like the snow outside. Who had set the fire in Chet's office? Could they flush out the shooter before he tried again? And where was Lou Duckworth hiding? How could there be two menaces running loose in the resort without leaving any clue as to their whereabouts? She mulled over these thoughts for a long time, her robe wrapped about her shoulders and the bedclothes pulled up to her chin. Finally, her eyes began to feel heavy.

She slid deeper under the covers. There was something wonderful about slipping down in bed, sleepy, relaxed, and ready to fall into sweet sleep.

She was sliding into a welcoming oblivion when a loud banging erupted at the door.

"Molly! Help!"

17

Molly's eyes flew open and she strained to see through the darkness. Who was at her door?

Angus immediately tunneled his way out from under the covers, doing his version of a growl as he came. Laura sat up, her confused grumbles mirroring Molly's.

The banging continued. "He's after me! Help!"

Molly climbed from the bed, grabbed her flashlight, and shined it at the door.

"Is that Paula?" Laura asked from the bed. "I thought she was sleeping in the den."

"Me too." Molly made her way to the door, a barking Angus at her side. "Coming," she called.

"Hurry! Please hurry." The last was a whimper.

Molly undid the security latch and turned the knob. The dead bolt released, and she opened the door.

Paula fell across the threshold into her arms. "Oh, Molly."

"What's wrong?" Molly asked.

"I heard him. He's down there." After all the yelling, Paula now whispered as if her pursuer might overhear her. She shook so hard that it was all Molly could do to hold on to her.

"Who's down there?"

"The gunman. Or that crazy photographer."

Molly heard doors opening up and down the hall. Trent was the first one to stick his head out. Chet came next, with Carol and Harvey a close third. The last, almost as alarmed as Paula, was Bobby. Flashlight beams splashed wildly around the hall.

"He almost got me." Paula flinched at the memory, bumping Molly's arm and sending her flashlight flying. It threw an arc of light across the hall before landing and casting a beam across Carol's feet, clad in a pair of Harvey's gray woolen hunting socks.

"Easy, Paula." Molly automatically patted her back, glancing over the woman's shoulder at an astonished Laura, who had lit the lantern on the bedside table.

"Please let me in." Full-blown hysteria gleamed in her eyes and bubbled in her voice.

"Of course." Molly backed up, taking Paula with her. "You're safe now." She paused to accept the flashlight Carol handed her, then she waved everyone back to bed. "We've got her. It's okay."

"I'll go check things out downstairs," Trent offered.

"Me too," Harvey volunteered, and the two men hurried off while the other doors closed.

Molly shut their door and flipped the security latch and the dead bolt, then she led Paula to the comfy chair and sat her down. She knelt in front of her. "Shh. It's okay. You're safe."

Paula leaned forward, her hands gripping each other hard enough that her knuckles were white in the low light of the room. She pushed her hands between her knees and rocked, eyes glassy.

Laura lit the second lantern to brighten the room as much as possible.

"Now, tell us what happened." Molly laid a hand on Paula's knee. "You were in the den?"

"I was," Paula said through chattering teeth. "When I fell asleep on the couch, the lights were on, the fire was burning, and I felt safe. Last night went so well, you know? I woke up to the lights off and the fire down to red coals. I was okay at first. I wasn't exactly happy because someone had switched off the lights on me, but I could see well enough. There was the red emergency light over the door as well as the glow from the fire, and I was nice and warm under the blankets."

"Sounds cozy." Laura sat on the floor beside Molly with Angus between them. He watched Paula curiously as if waiting for her explanation.

The young woman leaned forward, intent on her story. "Then I wondered why I woke up. Was it the cold? No, I was comfortable. A noise from the generator or something? No, all was the same. So, something else?" There was a dramatic pause, then Paula grabbed Molly's hand. "It was him!"

The effect was spot-on. Molly jumped. So did Laura. Angus gave a little yip of alarm.

"He was in the room with you?" Molly's mouth went dry at the thought.

"The shooter?" Laura's voice squeaked.

"No, not in the den, but he might as well have been," Paula said. "I could hear him moving around. Maybe he bumped into the wall or knocked something over. I'm not sure. All I knew was that I'd heard a thud. Then he dropped something. I heard it hit the floor, but I don't think it broke."

"Oh my," Laura murmured.

Paula focused on a spot over Molly's head as she spoke, apparently trying to remember it all. "I heard him mumbling to himself, but I couldn't make out any of the words. I heard another thud against the wall and a loud 'Ouch.'" Paula blinked herself back to the present. "I didn't know what to do. What if he came after me?"

What indeed. After another dramatic pause, Paula continued her story, and Molly knew beyond any doubt Paula had her father's innate ability with a story. She couldn't help making it exciting.

"I got out of bed—or rather, off the couch," she said. "Now I was standing in the middle of the room. I knew I couldn't stay there all night." She put her hand over her heart as she relived her terror. She might be overdramatizing, but her fear was genuine. Molly knew she'd have been scared witless in the same situation.

Paula swallowed. "I remembered you talking about where your room was. I thought if I could get to you, you could take me in and I'd be safe. I peered out the den door and couldn't see him, just the light shining under the door of the room next door."

Molly straightened. "Had the bumps and noise come from that room too?"

"Didn't I say that?" Paula asked.

"I thought you were talking about the hall," Molly said.

"No, next door. If he'd been in the hall, I'd still be in the den. Since I could still hear him bumping around behind the closed door, I slipped into the hall. I was afraid to use my flashlight. What if he saw it?"

"That would have been disastrous." Laura was hanging on every word.

"I started thinking, what if he opened the door as I went past? The very thought gave me the creeps, but I had to take the chance." Paula took a deep breath. "I ran down the hall, past the gym and the closed restaurants, and into that huge lobby. That is one scary room, let me tell you. I kept checking back over my shoulder, expecting to find him chasing me."

"Oh, Paula." Molly said again. She knew exactly who had been in the room next to the den, but she wasn't sure how to tell the frightened young woman.

"I raced across the lobby, scared of what was ahead but more afraid of what was behind. When I hit the stairwell, I switched on my flashlight and was sure he'd find me. Every sound is magnified in there."

Molly remembered how disconcerted she and Laura had felt in that stairwell the previous night, and they'd had each other and no one chasing them. Even tonight, with Trent and Chet for company, it had been eerie.

"So here I am." Paula turned pleading eyes on Molly and Laura. "Don't let him catch me."

Laura jumped to her feet. "We will protect you, I promise."

Molly was about to explain whom, exactly, Laura was protecting Paula from when there was another loud knock at the door.

"This is getting to be a habit," Laura said drily as she strode to the door.

Paula clutched her chest. "He's here."

"No." Molly patted her hands. "A bad guy wouldn't knock to announce his presence."

"It's too dark for the peephole." Laura opened the door cautiously, keeping the security latch in place. "It's Fergus." Relief filled her voice, and she opened the door fully.

"May I come in?" Fergus asked, dark circles under his eyes. "I need to speak to Paula."

Laura stepped back, and he went to the comfy chair and crouched in front of Paula.

"I hear you've had a bad night," he said.

Paula's eyes filled with tears. "Yes." It was more a hiccup than a word.

"I am so sorry."

"Thanks." She gave a tremulous smile. "But it wasn't your fault."

He grimaced apologetically. "I'm afraid it was. You see, the room next to the den is my office. It was me you heard. I was trying to catch up on some work."

Paula jerked back. "It was you?"

"I apologize," Fergus said. "I never considered you would hear me."

Paula blinked, clearly processing the fact that she'd never been in danger. "There was no one after me?"

Fergus shook his head.

Anger surfaced in her expression. "You scared me to death!" She stuck her finger in his face. "How could you? I was terrified!"

He put his hands up in surrender.

She blew out a huge puff of air, then flopped against the chair back. "Don't do it again."

Molly gave Fergus a small smile. "I assume Trent and Harvey alerted you to the situation up here?"

"They did." Fergus stood. "You've had a rough time at Castleglen, Paula, but you can rest assured that no one is going to hurt you."

"You promise?" Paula said.

Molly watched Fergus with interest. How would he answer this without lying? He really couldn't guarantee her safety—or anyone else's for that matter. The shooter still roamed the halls, though Paula was a most unlikely target. The fact remained that a gunman was loose, and since they didn't know who it was or what he wanted, no one was truly safe.

"We've got two action heroes and a very competent police officer with us," Fergus said smoothly. "To say nothing of the others here who will do their best for you, Paula. You don't know this, but Molly and Laura regularly chase down bad guys."

Paula was fascinated. "Really?"

"Really. They'll have to tell you some of their stories." Fergus smiled. "Now get a good night's sleep. The storm's supposed to lessen by late tomorrow afternoon. We should be out of here some time the day after. This will all be over before you know it."

She began absently plaiting her hair, but she managed a slight lift at the corners of her mouth. "Okay."

Molly accompanied Fergus to the door while Laura and Angus stayed with Paula.

"Are you okay, Molly?" he asked.

She gave him her best smile. He slid an arm around her, and she dropped her head to his shoulder for a quick moment of comfort. "As soon as she said the noise came from the room next to the den, I knew what was going on."

"I feel bad for frightening her, but I know she's in good hands." Fergus stepped into the hall.

She caught his hand. "You aren't going back to work, are you? You're so weary."

"No more work tonight." He gave her a quick hug. "See you in the morning." He disappeared into his room.

Molly latched the door once again, then returned to the still-jumpy Paula.

"I can't tell you how scared I was." Paula hugged herself. "And it was only Fergus."

"I'd say you did a great job taking care of yourself in a bad situation," Laura said.

"You certainly did," Molly chimed in. "Lots of people would have disappeared under the covers and spent the night shaking and crying."

"That's right," Laura agreed. "You escaped. You refused to cower. If it had been the bad guy down there, you would have bested him."

Molly could practically see the thoughts evolving as Paula eyed them thoughtfully, the idea that she'd been brave replacing the idea that she'd been a victim.

The young woman inhaled deeply, almost visibly sloughing off stress. Her gaze sharpened. "Who saw me screaming and yelling outside your door?"

Molly could tell the answer mattered to her. "No one important. All the other Californians have rooms upstairs, remember?"

Frowning, Paula glanced at the door, then bit her lip. She opened her mouth to say something, but stopped.

"Would you like to sleep here?" Molly asked. "You can have the pullout."

"You mean it?" Paula's eyes lit up.

"The more the merrier," Laura said.

A short while later, everyone had snuggled down into their beds. As Molly drew the covers close again, she willed her mind to shut off. She needed all the energy she could muster for whatever surprises might meet her tomorrow.

Morning arrived with the wind still snarling and the snow still piling ever higher. The lure of the warm den waiting downstairs helped Molly dress quickly in several layers of fleece and wool.

"Angus needs his walk," she told Laura and Paula as she grabbed her flashlight for the trip through the powerless wing. "We'll see you downstairs."

Molly held the door open and Angus scooted through. She pushed the stairwell door open, her flashlight spearing into the darkness of the windowless area. "Come on, Angus," she said as she entered the vestibule. "Down we go."

But then she froze at a sight she had never expected.

18

Caught in Molly's flashlight beam was a short, slim, slightly stooped man with wrinkled clothes, an unshaven jaw, and uncombed hair. A camera with a long lens hung around his neck, and it swung heavily as he whirled and ran back up the stairs to the third floor.

Molly shrieked in surprise and took a step. Her foot hit the edge of a stair, more than half off the tread. She felt her ankle fold. She gave a pain-filled gasp as her leg gave way beneath her.

She tumbled down the steps, her hands scrabbling for something to stop her fall. She scrabbled for the railing, her only hope. Her fingers curled around the barrier, and she clamped tight, holding on with all her might. She gripped as gravity tried to pull her down to slam on the cement landing below.

Even as her hands held fast, her body was in freefall. Her legs caught up with her upper body and slid past it, her injured ankle thumping against a step's edge on the way. She twisted, trying to gain control, and instead slammed against the railing supports. Her breath rushed out of her lungs, and pain sliced through her. The pull of her own weight wrenched her arms, making her shoulders scream.

She hung there, trying to get her mind around what had just happened, trying to get her feet beneath her.

"Are you okay?" A beam shined in her face.

Was she? Good question. She blinked against the bright light.

She put her left foot on a step and pain rocketed up her leg. She took the weight off immediately and tried her other foot. Fortunately, that one was okay. Clutching the railing for balance, she settled herself on a stair.

She took a deep breath. Her heart was still racketing in her chest, and she was still shaking inside, but she felt the world slowly begin to right itself. She rested her head on her bent knee. Her left leg hung over a step with no pressure on its ankle.

Angus pushed against her, his little body quivering. She could feel his distress. She ran a hand down his back. "It's okay, buddy. I'm okay."

He sat beside her, his chin resting on her thigh. She stroked him as much to soothe herself as him.

"Goodness, you scared me." The voice came from behind the beam, and she squinted toward the speaker.

"Lou Duckworth?" she managed.

"That's me," he said. "I'm so sorry. I'd never do anything to hurt anyone."

"You wouldn't shoot them?"

He patted his camera. "Shooting people is what I do."

Molly lifted her left leg and rested her foot on the step. Pain grabbed her again, centering on her ankle. After she caught her breath, she said, "With a gun, I mean."

"A gun?"

Molly couldn't see his expression with the beam of his flashlight in her eyes, but he sounded shocked.

"Yes, a gun. Did you shoot Adam?" Where was her flashlight? She searched wildly and saw it resting on the landing where she could have wound up in a tangled, broken mess. It sent its light uselessly into the far corner.

"Adam Lorbetski was shot?" Duckworth collapsed on the step beside her. "Is he . . . dead?" The answer mattered to him. Molly could hear it in his voice, feel it in his intensity.

"No, thank goodness. He's in the hospital, where he's fighting for his life." She raised an eyebrow. "How could you not know about it? There were police and an ambulance."

"Here? When?"

"Monday afternoon, just as the storm began."

He scratched his head. "I guess I was in my room trying to figure out how to stay one step ahead of all of you."

"Right." Molly's hands hurt, and she shook them, opening and closing her fists. Her shoulders ached too. She windmilled her arms forward and backward, and her shoulders moved easily if painfully. "How's that working out for you?"

"Not so well, thanks to you," he said with a huff. "First my comfy room, then the storage closet."

She shot him a glare. "You were watching us. That's creepy."

"I watch people for a living." Lou said it with pride.

"I know, especially Rocky. He hates the invasion of his privacy. You know that, but you still do it."

"It's the price he pays for that fat paycheck he takes home."

"And the price you pay is trouble with the law for stalking?"

"I don't stalk." He sounded truly offended. "Stalkers have bad motives. I don't."

"No guilt?"

"No guilt."

Molly had no response to that, so she gave herself a more thorough once-over and decided that her internal shaking was gone, her heartbeat steady, and it was time to get on with her day. She grabbed the railing and tried to pull herself upright using one leg. She ended up back on the step. "You're going to have to help me, Lou."

"I'll get you to your feet, then I'm gone."

"You'd leave me here in the dark?"

"Someone will be along soon." The flashlight beam shifted, and he held out his hand.

Angus jumped to his feet, barking animatedly.

Lou yanked his hand back. "Will he bite me?"

Instead of answering, she listened as far-off voices and the thud of a guest room door closing filtered into the stairwell. "Laura and Paula are coming," she said. "That's probably why he's barking."

The voices got louder and the stairwell door flew open. Angus rushed to Laura, jumping to put his paws on her leg and issuing urgent doggie cries.

Laura bent and scratched his head. "What are you doing here, Angus?" she asked. "You're supposed to be downstairs."

Paula ran her flashlight over the area, and the beam came to rest on Molly. "Molly! What are you doing here in the dark?"

"I fell." Molly was embarrassed to hear her voice shake.

Laura gasped. "What?"

The two women rushed to her while Angus barked his concern.

Paula crouched in front of Molly. She handed her flashlight to Laura. "Here. Hold this."

Laura automatically took it, a light in each hand. "What happened?"

Paula waved away that question and concentrated on Molly. "What hurts?"

"My left ankle," Molly answered.

"I'm going to take off your shoe and sock. Okay?" Ditzy Paula had disappeared, and a calm, competent woman had taken her place. If Molly hadn't felt dizzy already, the change would have made her head spin.

Paula removed the sock and shoe and set them aside. She began a gentle probing. "Do you hurt anywhere else?"

Molly gave a little laugh. "All over, but nothing serious."

"Did you bump your head?"

"No."

"You're sure?"

"I'm sure. It's my ankle." And her shoulders. And her arms. And her hands, and her hip where it had met the stair. But they were general aches, the kind that hurt for a few days but slowly disappeared, the kind that left bruises but no permanent damage.

"What kind of pain here?" Paula was back to probing the ankle. "Stabbing, aching, throbbing?"

"It's not too bad if I don't move it or put pressure on it. Then it feels like a stabbing pain. Otherwise it's a consistent ache."

"On a scale of one to ten, what's the consistent ache like?"

"Maybe a three."

"Can you stand?"

"On one leg, if someone gives me a hand up." At that, Molly noticed that Lou had vanished.

"How did you fall?" Laura asked.

"I opened the door, and he was right there," Molly said. "He scared me."

"Who?" Laura and Paula asked in unison.

"Lou Duckworth. I knew it was him because he had his camera on a strap around his neck."

"He's here?" Laura scanned the empty stairwell.

"He was," Molly said. "When I opened the door, I don't know which of us was more scared. He turned to run. I stepped wrong and twisted my ankle."

Laura grumbled something under her breath. "And he just left you here?"

Molly shook her head. "He stayed until you two came."

Paula stood. "We need to get you to the den to check you out where I can actually see." She took her flashlight from Laura and ran its beam all over Molly. "You're not bleeding anywhere, but that ankle concerns me. Do you think you can scoot down the stairs? That might be safer than Laura and me trying to help you climb down stairs in the dark."

"Better safe than falling again." Molly agreed. With the encouragement of both women and the close presence of Angus, she slid down step by step.

When they arrived at the landing, Laura retrieved Molly's flashlight. She stuck it in Molly's shoe, which she'd grabbed from upstairs. "I'll hang on to these for you."

"You're going to have to," Molly said. "I need both hands."

They rounded the landing and continued down the final flight.

Molly stopped two steps from the bottom. "You know, if I don't move my ankle, it really doesn't hurt too much." But no sooner had she spoken than Angus brushed against the ankle and she cried out.

"Okay," Paula said. "Laura and I are going to help you stand. We're going to get on either side of you, wrap our arms beneath your armpits and up your back, and we're going to lift. You're going to help push with your good leg."

In no time, they had Molly upright, balanced on her right leg, her left bent behind her. She draped an arm about each woman, and they hobbled their way across the lobby, stopping at the front door for Angus to make a quick dash outside. They moved on to the den, Angus trotting beside them. Laura flipped on the room's lights.

Molly sank gratefully onto one of the couches. Her hands ached, and her shoulders hurt from the strain of walking one-legged.

Laura grabbed one of Molly's hands and flipped it palm up. It was red and sore-looking. "Oh, Molly."

"That's from holding onto the rail so I wouldn't fall," Molly explained.

Paula took the other hand carefully. Her touch was soft but firm.

"It's pretty bruised. Hold a cold compress and they'll feel a lot better. And you'll need a new manicure. You've got a couple of broken nails."

"Exactly how close did you get to falling down those steps, Molly?" Laura asked.

Molly gave a shudder as she remembered.

"I suspect that you'll have a sore back and shoulders from what must have been a terrible wrenching," Paula warned her.

Molly had no doubt.

Paula focused on Molly's ankle once more. "You need R.I.C.E. Rest, ice, compression, and elevation. Let's get started with the rest. Lie down."

"I can't," Molly protested. "I have to help with breakfast."

"Not today you don't." Laura gave her a gentle push.

Molly fell back with a groan. "I can't have a bad ankle. I have too much to do."

"Laura, would you please get an ice pack from Chet's office refrigerator?" Paula asked it as a question but it was unmistakably an order. "And check the first aid kit for an elastic bandage."

Laura aimed her index finger at Molly. "Don't go anywhere."

As Laura left the room, Paula spotted her beautiful boots where she'd abandoned them the previous night. With a little cry of delight, she ran to them. She dropped onto what had been her bed and pulled them on. She stuck out her foot. "Aren't they the best?"

"They really are." Molly pushed herself up on her elbows, only to drop down again. Putting the strain on her shoulders hurt. "Can you get me a pillow?"

Paula's competent side reappeared. "Of course." She began rounding up the decorative pillows strewn artistically about the room. "Compression will have to wait until we get you a bandage, so we'll skip right to the E and elevate."

She slid a pillow beneath Molly's head and stacked three more at the far end of the couch. She gently placed Molly's foot on top. "The idea is for your foot to be higher than your heart."

Laura returned shortly with an ice pack, though she hadn't been able to find a bandage. Paula was placing the ice pack on Molly's ankle when Greer and the Sinclairs entered. Greer immediately gave Molly a careful examination, having taken many first aid courses in her police training. But when Molly reported having seen Lou, Greer quickly took off to search for him, Rocky on her heels.

A few minutes later, Chet came in and performed his own exam. "We gym managers have to know all kinds of first aid," he explained. "Sprained and broken ankles are a dime a dozen. I've got lots of elastic bandages." He disappeared to get one.

Molly sat up when Chet returned. He wrapped her ankle while Paula watched over his shoulder. When he finished, Paula carefully slipped Molly's sock back on to keep her foot warm.

"Now lay back again, Molly," Paula ordered. "Get that foot raised." She adjusted the ice and draped a blanket over Molly's legs.

Chet scooted Jonathan's chair away from the fireplace so that Molly would receive the blaze's full effect. Despite the care she was shown, sitting there while everyone else moved around on their two sound legs made Molly grumpy. She hated not being able to help. She hated being the one needing help. The fact that Laura and Carol, with help from Adrian and Paula, made and served breakfast without missing her didn't do much for her mood. She knew she was being foolish, and that made her grouchier.

As she told herself she should be grateful that all she'd suffered was a bad ankle, Fergus came over with a cup of coffee and a plate of pancakes and bacon. He set them on the floor and helped her sit higher with a couple more pillows behind her back, all the while keeping her leg raised. She basked in his thoughtfulness.

When she was situated, he gave her the plate of food. "I'll be back in a minute." He strode back to the food tables.

Suddenly, Angus and Hero were beside her, eyeing the bacon that was as close to their level as could be.

"Shoo," she said.

They didn't move. Hero licked his chops.

"Help," she mumbled, but no one heard her.

Laura was talking with Trent, Carol and Harvey were talking with Adrian, and Trace was studying his phone screen. Paula sat with Chet, her legs crossed and one aqua boot bouncing up and down.

Fergus reappeared and sat on the floor beside her. He had a plate of food for himself and utensils and napkins for two. "Here you go." He gave her a set.

"Thank you." Her eyes filled with tears of gratitude at the simple gesture, a sure sign that she was more shaken than she'd thought.

He saw them. "Tell me about it," he said, so she did. When she finished, he asked, "And Duckworth went up?"

"Yes. Greer already ran off to search for him."

"We'll join her after breakfast. Now take these." He handed her a couple of over-the-counter painkillers. "They'll help you feel better."

The pills did help the ache to subside, and the food elevated her mood. Or was it the handsome man who sat beside her?

Unfortunately, a more pressing matter called, and Fergus left her to search Castleglen for Lou Duckworth with the others. Molly remained alone in front of the fire with only Angus and Hero to keep her company.

The snow still beat against the windows, blown by great gusts of wind that made the entire resort creak eerily. Seeking comfort, Molly patted the couch, and Angus climbed up beside her. Hero tried to climb up too, his puppy clumsiness making her laugh. Eventually, the three of them found equilibrium.

Until Molly realized she had a big problem.

In all the days they'd been at the resort, Molly hadn't thought much about the short distance between the den and the ladies' room down the hall. Now, though, the journey felt epic.

She took a deep breath. There was nothing for it. She had to rise.

She swung her injured foot off the pillows and lowered both feet to the floor. The dogs sat up, blinking, taking it personally that she had disturbed their sleep. She gave them each a pat and slid to the edge of the couch. With a push, she stood, all her weight on her right foot. Just the toe of her left foot touched the ground, enough to ensure she wouldn't topple over.

Her ankle hurt more with gravity pulling the blood to it, a dull steady ache. She tried to put weight on it, and the pain became stabbing. She had to grab the arm of the couch to keep from falling.

"I have to try," she told the dogs, who watched her with interest. "It should be frozen from the ice pack, so you'd think it wouldn't hurt, right?"

The dogs reserved judgment.

She put weight on the ball of her bad foot. It hurt, but not like when she set her foot flat. She took a step. It was extremely uncomfortable, but not impossible. It was staying put and doing nothing that was impossible. She limped to the door and paused.

"Stay," she told the dogs, her hand held out. "I won't be long."

They gave her that woebegone expression dogs did so well, but she bet they'd be back to napping before she was down the hall.

She limped past a couple of conference rooms to the ladies' room. By the time she emerged, she was hurting big time. She studied the distant den door and wondered how it could seem so far away.

Unless she wanted to sit in the hall and wait for the searchers to return, there was no help for it. Resigned, she began the long trek.

Something caught her attention. She stopped and listened. A noise came from the small conference room she was passing. Before she could talk herself out of it, she grabbed the door handle. She expected the room to be locked, but the knob gave way under her hand. She tugged the door open a crack, just enough to peek inside.

A long, highly polished wooden table sat in the center of the room, twelve equally polished chairs surrounding it. The first abnormal thing she noted was that the room's lights were on. The second was one of the chairs was angled away from the table while the others were neatly pushed in. The third was a camera strap sticking out from under the skirting on a serving table set against the side wall.

She pulled the door all the way open and went in. "How in the world did you get here without being seen?"

There was no answer.

She limped to the table, pulled out a chair and sat. "I know you're under that table, Lou. Your camera strap is sticking out."

The strap disappeared.

She pulled out a second chair and carefully lifted her poor aching foot to rest on it. The move might not put her foot above her heart, but it was better than it being on the floor. "I suppose I'll sit here and wait for you," she said. "I've got all the time in the world."

She heard a heavy sigh, then the table skirt lifted, and Lou crawled out. He climbed to his feet, his camera dangling from his hand. He managed a weary smile. "How's the foot?"

"Quite painful," Molly answered as Lou walked to the table and slid into the angled chair. "Aren't you going to run away again? I can't chase you."

"Where can I run? Your friends are everywhere I go."

Molly shifted in her seat, trying to ease the ache. "So you're going to give yourself up?"

Lou made a face that appeared to be a mixture of frustration that he'd run out of options and resignation to his fate. "At least I got a couple of great pictures of Rocky and that girl." He leaned in. "Who is she, Molly? Come on, tell me. What's her name? What does she do?"

"Oh no." Molly shook her head. "Not a chance."

"I'll give you a cut of the money I'll make for the picture with her name beside Rocky's. Believe me, that's not a figure to sneeze at."

Molly tried to decide if she should be offended or flattered. "Are you offering me a bribe?"

Lou laughed. "I guess it depends on how you look at it. I meant it as a business deal, honorable man that I am."

"Molly!" Carol's worried voice echoed down the hall. "Where are you?"

"In the little conference room," Molly called back.

Running footsteps approached, and then Carol burst through the door, talking as she came. "I got worried about you being alone, so I came to check on you and see if you needed anything. What are you doing in here?" Then she saw Lou and came to an abrupt halt. "What—?"

Molly waved a hand. "Carol, this is Lou Duckworth."

Carol sank into a chair. "They're all searching for you."

Lou hummed acknowledgment.

"Molly? Where are you?" Apprehension crackled in the voice in the hall.

Carol rose and leaned out the door. "Down here, Laura."

"What's she doing in there?" Laura sailed into the room. "Molly, what are you—?" She froze when she saw Lou.

Paula came charging into the room. "Molly, what are you doing off the couch?"

"Hello, Paula," Lou said.

Paula stopped cold, folded her arms, and glared at the man. "You've really done it this time, Uncle Lou."

19

Lou grinned at Paula. "Oh, come on, sweetheart. You loved it."

Paula started fiddling with her hair. "Those were some impressive pictures."

"You know it," Lou said. "No doubt Sol is singing your praises."

"But I didn't do anything," the young woman protested.

Lou shrugged. "Maybe he doesn't know that. Nor does he need to."

"Wait." Molly stared at the girl. "Lou is your uncle?"

"My mother's brother," Paula said. "It's a well-kept family secret."

"You know I'm your favorite uncle," Lou put in.

Paula sent him a frown. "It depends on the day. The last couple haven't been your finest. Daddy would be apoplectic."

"Her father likes to pretend I don't exist," Lou explained to Molly. "I'm an embarrassment."

Paula crossed the room and sat beside Lou. She took his hand. "You have to give up on Rocky, Uncle Lou."

A crafty expression washed over his features. "Maybe I could go out in a blaze of glory if I could reveal the name of his new romantic interest. You know, be the first to tell the world. I'd make sure your name was on the credit line."

Molly opened her mouth to protest, but Paula didn't need coaching.

"Uncle Lou, you should be ashamed."

Lou sat back in his chair and gazed sadly at Paula. "You know, kid, you're too good for this business."

"I don't know about that," Molly said. "But I do think her talents lie elsewhere."

"Me too," Laura put in. "You should have seen her take amazing care of Molly."

Paula seemed floored. "You thought I was good?"

"Paula, you were great," Laura said firmly.

"How did you know exactly what to do?" Molly wondered briefly if they were finally about to figure this girl out.

Paula shot a glance at Lou as if she didn't feel brave enough to speak in front of him.

"You're like two people," Laura observed. "There's the tentative girl who acts as if she can't make decisions or accept challenges, the one who plays with her hair to cover her uncertainties. Then on the other hand, there's the competent, take-charge Paula who steps up when there's a need, the one who knows how to help people and enjoys doing it."

"Which one is the real Paula?" Molly asked.

With all eyes trained on her, Paula blinked against tears. "I don't know."

Silence fell as everyone took in that tortured whisper. Molly shifted in her seat, seeking a more comfortable position for her foot, for her whole aching body.

Paula noticed and jumped up. "We can talk about me later. We need to take you back to the den and get that leg elevated again. Laura, help me walk her there like we did before."

Laura stood. "Yes ma'am. Molly, where would you like us to take you?"

Molly held out her hands. "I'd love the couch again—and another dose of aspirin."

Molly saw Lou's eyes dart to his camera and sent a significant look Carol's way.

Her friend immediately caught on and grabbed the camera. "I'll carry this."

Lou narrowed his eyes at her audacity.

Carol smiled sweetly at him. "I've been married for decades. I've spent those years staring down a tougher man than you'll ever be."

"Maybe I'll simply take it from you and run," Lou taunted.

"Run where? You're caught and you know it." Carol opened the door for Molly and her human crutches.

Lou's shoulders sagged as he followed them out, flicking off the lights as he went.

Once Molly was settled on her couch, Paula headed for the coffee bar. It was obvious that she regretted her earlier openness and wanted to discourage any more questions.

Molly faced the fire and enjoyed the warmth. She wasn't sure what to say to repair the broken conversation thread. It had been important and revelatory, but intrusion into the private life of someone she barely knew felt rude, to say nothing of awkward. "Could you please make me a cup of peppermint tea too, Paula?"

"Um, sure." Paula fiddled with the tea wrapper in her hand.

Lou had none of Molly's hesitation. "Okay, Paula. Forget the tea. Come talk to me. What do these women mean that there are two Paulas? I've only ever seen the cute, slightly ditzy one. I love that Paula, but I do worry about her lack of purpose, her inability to stick with anything."

"You've never seen her in an emergency." Laura spoke with certainty.

"No, I haven't," Lou admitted.

"You should," Laura replied. "She's amazing."

Paula flushed under the praise.

"Did you go to college, Paula?" Molly asked.

"One semester. Dad wanted me to go to film school at UCLA." She shrugged. "I had fun, but it didn't feel like the right fit."

"But I'm guessing you don't want to be involved in film." Carol pulled a chair close to Molly's couch. "Am I right?"

Paula's expression was pained. "Everyone I know is involved in film. It's their lives."

"That's fine for them," Molly said. "But if you don't feel the drive, the compulsion to be part of the film community, then don't be. You already told me you don't like your job as a publicist."

"Sol is so pushy," Paula said, flopping down on the love seat beside Lou.

Laura sat on the arm of the couch. "It's not Sol, Paula. You're a round peg trying to squeeze yourself into a square hole because everyone else around you fits into that hole."

"We're all born with certain talents," Carol said. "When we discover and follow these built-in gifts, we are a lot happier. We're doing what we were created to do, being who we're created to be."

Paula's expression was part deer in the headlights and part hope.

Lou grabbed her hands. "Forget these ladies, smart as they are. Forget your old man and your mom. Forget Sol. Tell Uncle Lou the truth. What do you want to do? What makes you happy?"

"I . . . um . . ." Paula was struggling to spit it out.

Lou patted her hand. "I can't believe I've never asked you that before. I'm as bad as your father—which makes my stomach hurt. You can tell me, sweetheart. What do you like?"

Paula studied their joined hands. "I like to help people." Her voice was breathy as if making this confession took all her nerve.

"That's wonderful," Lou said. "Give me specifics. How do you like to help people?"

"By making them feel better," she said.

"I like to make them feel happy too." He grinned. "A good picture makes people happy."

"Not feel happy," Paula corrected. "Feel better. Get better. As in healing. Maybe even"—she hesitated and took a deep breath—"saving lives."

Bingo, Molly thought.

"Like being a nurse or something?" Lou appeared utterly gobsmacked.

It was as if Paula had come to life for the first time. "I love all these real-life rescue documentaries and all the doctor shows, not for the story lines but for the diseases and the medical stuff. I watch videos online of EMTs and rescue squads and firefighters in the field. I read everything I can find about what to do when bad things happen. I love books about catastrophes and rescues." She blushed. "Nobody knew that until now. It's my secret." At Lou's expression of disbelief, the light in her eyes went out. She pulled her hands free and began finger combing her hair. "It's dumb, I know. There's no way I could be someone like that."

Lou gaped at her. Molly wanted to shake him. *Say something!*

Instead of speaking, he grabbed her and hugged her. Paula hugged him back and began to cry.

Into this emotional moment walked Rocky and Greer, deep in conversation.

If Laura, Carol, and Paula had been surprised to see Lou, Rocky and Greer were stunned. They stood just inside the door, staring at the man, their half-finished sentences trailing off.

Lou ignored them. He sat back from Paula and patted her gently on the cheek. "You be you, sweetheart. Forget the rest of us. Be you. Be a rescuer, whatever kind you want."

Paula's expression was both terrified and hopeful. "Daddy will hate it."

"Tough. It's your life, not his." Lou gave a crooked smile. "Don't worry. When he hears we've talked, he'll find some way to blame me for your independence."

Paula threw her arms around his neck. "I love you, Uncle Lou.

You drive me crazy, but I love you. I want to be strong like you and follow my heart."

Lou blinked. "I don't think anyone's ever complimented me for being hardheaded before."

Greer woke from her shock and stalked across the room. "He's not a good role model, Paula."

Paula grinned. "I know, but he's the best I've got."

"Hey!" Lou feigned offense. "I don't think taking a few pictures is all that bad."

"Maybe not if you're invited to do so." Greer glared at him. "But skulking around in the dark and taking advantage of someone?"

Molly wasn't sure whether she meant herself or Rocky.

Greer went on. "And then there's breaking and entering. And trespassing. Harassment."

Lou appraised Greer with interest. "You're prettier up close. No wonder Rocky's smitten."

"Back off, Lou." Rocky glowered at the photographer. "It's bad enough I have to fight with you. Greer is off-limits."

"But I made her famous." Lou said it as though she should be grateful.

Greer flushed red with anger. "I don't want to be famous!"

"Why not?" Lou asked. "There's money in being famous."

Fergus came in, then held the door for Chet, who was holding a pair of aluminum crutches. "Hey, Molly. Look what I found. I forgot I had them." He offered them to her.

"Thanks, Chet. These will definitely come in handy," Molly said, grateful that she would no longer have to use Laura and Paula as human crutches.

Adrian, Trace, and Bobby entered, and Adrian headed straight for the coffee bar, grumbling, "I'm starting to feel the cold in my bones."

"Hello, Adrian." Lou gave a little wave.

Adrian shut his eyes as if blocking Lou from existence. "Who found him?"

"Molly," Laura and Carol said together.

While Molly shared her story about finding Lou, Trace took the dogs out, and Laura and Carol went to the kitchen to work on lunch. Greer determined that the photographer could remain in the den for the duration of the storm. After that, they'd decide exactly what to do about him.

Lou was settling in a corner of the den as far from Rocky and Adrian's withering glares as possible when Trace came back, expression grouchy. "It is *nasty* out there."

Molly gave Angus a quick hug when he jumped up beside her again. She ignored his wet feet and fur, knowing they'd dry quickly this close to the fire.

Trace slouched down on the floor beside Molly's couch, Hero by his side. "Will this ever stop?" He glared at the window and the wild weather.

Molly thought she perceived a slackening of the snow's density and an easing of the wind, both good signs. "They say it should be over sometime this afternoon."

"Then what?" he grumbled. "Are we snowed in until summer?"

"You'll love summer here."

"I doubt it."

"It's warm and sunny with lots of outdoor activities. The days are long." She smiled broadly. "It's great."

He was visibly unimpressed. "Have you always lived here?"

"I grew up farther south in Ann Arbor, and I lived in Chicago for many years."

"That's cold too, isn't it? But at least there's stuff to do there."

"Yes, Chicago was a lot of fun."

"So why'd you leave there and come to the middle of nowhere?"

"I love it here." Molly laughed at Trace's expression of disbelief. "Laura used to live in New York City. Carol and Harvey lived near Pittsburgh."

"And they moved here." *Here* was clearly the end of the earth.

"We all love it."

"Well, I hate it." Trace had his arms clamped so tightly around Hero that the dog protested. Hero wiggled out of the boy's grasp but rearranged himself to rest his head on Trace's leg as if he intuited his agitation. "It's always dark, and it snows and snows, and it's boring, and I want to go home."

"When the storm passes, the sun will sparkle on the snow. It'll be so bright you'll need sunglasses. And it will be beautiful."

He snorted in disbelief.

"And of course it's boring. That's part of being snowed in. It makes us appreciate getting back to life as usual."

"My life is in California, not here."

"There are plenty of kids your age who live here, you know. And the high school is really nice."

Rocky sat on the floor beside Trace. "I'm not sure telling him about school is the best way to make him eager to settle in Loch Mallaig." He shoulder bumped Trace.

Trace gave his brother a sour face and climbed to his feet, disrupting Hero. "Nothing will make me eager to live here. Nothing!" He stomped away to stare out the window.

Rocky watched Trace go with a slight smile on his lips. "Did you see that, Adrian?"

"I sure did," Adrian confirmed. "A bit feisty, wouldn't you say?"

"Wonderful, wouldn't you say?"

Adrian grinned back at his older nephew. "Three times since we've been here, he's shown uncharacteristic spunk. He rescued Hero and was willing to defy you to keep him. He went in the hot tub against our advice, though with our cooperation. And he just lost his temper with no intention of apologizing."

Rocky laughed. "I know he's going to drive me crazy when he gets the hang of this standing up for himself, but right now, I couldn't be happier. This is the place to be."

"I agree," Adrian said. "The ability to have his own opinions and stand up for them has been buried under all the insecurities he's developed from losing his parents and being left with caregivers too much."

Rocky stared at the ground. "My fault, and my responsibility to fix."

"What else could you have done?" Adrian asked. When Rocky shrugged, he went on, "Don't blame yourself, Rock. Life circumstances are what they are, and you have always done the best you could for him. The kid may be thirteen and have to deal with the pressure of having a famous family, but he's coming along. You're going to save him yet." Adrian beamed.

"And probably get ulcers in the process."

"Like any parent of a teen."

Greer listened to this conversation with an approving light in her eyes.

Jonathan stalked into the room. He started toward his usual seat by the fire and drew up short when he saw Molly laid out on the couch with her ankle raised and his chair several feet farther from the fireplace than he'd left it.

"I sprained my ankle," Molly explained, and disdain flashed across his face.

"Jonathan." Rocky stood, and Jonathan stiffened as if expecting another confrontation. "Greer and I would like to speak with you if you have a minute."

Jonathan was taken off guard by the request. He studied Rocky as if waiting for the trick. When none came, he said hesitantly, "Sure."

The three settled in chairs not far from Molly, who couldn't help but overhear their fascinating conversation.

"We have a proposal we'd like to run past you," Rocky said.

"You want me to evaluate a proposal?" Jonathan's surprise shimmered in the air.

"Business is business," Rocky said, his tone casual. "Personal is personal."

There was a silence, and it took all Molly's self-control not to spin around to see Jonathan's expression.

Rocky continued, "Greer and I have been talking about a TV series about a pair of cops in a small Michigan town, and—"

Jonathan interrupted. "What would make it different from all the many cop shows out there?"

Rocky grinned his million-dollar smile. "Me."

Jonathan sputtered a bit before saying, "Why do you want to do a TV series?"

"I can stay in one spot, hopefully here," Rocky explained. "I'm not going anywhere for a while after we settle in Michigan. Trace needs me with him whether he knows it or not. So if we could film here—"

Jonathan made a choking sound. "Are you kidding?"

"It's great here most of the time." Greer spoke up to defend her town. "You could film spring, summer, and fall."

"And I suppose you want to play the female cop to Rocky's hero?" Jonathan's tone was resigned.

"What?" Greer's horror at that idea of her acting was loud and clear. "No. Never."

"She would be a technical advisor," Rocky said. "Your job is to make all this happen, Jonathan."

Before Molly heard Jonathan's answer—but really, how could he say no?—Chet materialized beside her and gestured toward the crutches, which were propped against the arm of the sofa. "It's time for your lessons."

Unhappily, Molly pulled herself to her feet and stuffed the crutches under her arms. Chet adjusted them for her height, then led her to the hallway. For the next fifteen minutes, she struggled back and forth, Chet walking beside her as a spotter.

When she collapsed in an easy chair outside the ladies' room, exhausted from her trial by crutches, she glared at the supports. "Those things are devices of torture."

Chet leaned them against the wall behind her. "I know, but they work. Grab them any time you need to move around. It'll get easier with practice. I guarantee it."

She let her skepticism show. "Not that I doubt your word, but..."

With a laugh he indicated the buffet table, which was now loaded with the latest offerings. "Want me to fix you a plate?"

"You go ahead," she said. "I'll make my way." As soon as Chet left to join the line, though, Molly's stomach rumbled at the delicious aromas wafting down the hall. She was wondering how she'd carry a plate while using crutches when Fergus emerged from his office and helped her get settled at the dining table in the den with bowls of Adrian's loaded potato soup and Laura's chopped salad. Carol had made an angel food cake, light and airy after the heavy meal.

After lunch Molly hobbled her way back to the couch while Fergus returned to work, and most everyone else went to exercise or at least get a change of scenery elsewhere in the resort. Carol and Laura lingered in the den with paperbacks.

Weary and sated, Molly lay back and closed her eyes, trying to nap. Though dulled by painkillers, the throbbing in her ankle kept her just uncomfortable enough to prevent sleep. Instead, her thoughts pinballed around the mysterious gunman. She'd found Lou hiding, but he certainly didn't seem a likely suspect. In that case, the shooter was still hiding in the resort—or was it one of the guests?

Molly frowned as she contemplated that. Jonathan was the obvious choice considering his consistently sour demeanor, but she wasn't sure what he'd gain from Rocky's death. Was he vindictive enough to kill a client because he thought he might make less money?

Next, Molly considered Paula. The girl was quite the mystery—and if she'd managed to keep the secret that Lou was her uncle, what other secrets might she be keeping? Growing up in Hollywood, she might have some longtime grudge against Rocky that nobody would guess. Had he snubbed her studio-head father in some way? Or had he slighted her, perhaps dismissing romantic advances?

It's too bad Bobby didn't see the shooter in the gym. That would make this all a lot easier. Realizing she wasn't making any headway trying to figure out the shooter's identity, Molly forced herself to set the idea aside. Instead, she focused on the victim. If Rocky was the target, Greer had kept him out of harm's way enough that the shooter hadn't made another attempt on his life. But if Rocky wasn't the intended victim . . .

Molly's eyes flew open.

She had figured it out.

20

Molly zeroed in on Carol and Laura, who were seated on an adjacent love seat. No one else had returned, so they were alone for the moment. "Ladies," Molly said. "I think I know our shooter's target."

"You do?" Carol asked, lowering her book.

Molly took a deep breath while she made sure she had her thoughts aligned. "Think with me a minute. Who was at the first shooting?"

"Rocky, Adam, and Chet," Laura said, glancing to Carol for agreement.

"And the second?" Molly pressed.

"Rocky, Trace, and Chet." Laura shivered. "I was there."

"Now who would be hurt by the fire in Chet's office?"

"Chet obviously," Carol said.

"And Fergus." Laura sat straight. "He wouldn't be hurt physically, but there would have been damage to Chet's desk and computer and such. That's a financial cost to Fergus."

"And who would be hurt by the window breaking?" Molly prompted.

Carol frowned. "Again, no one would be hurt physically, but Fergus could have been hurt financially if he had to replace that floor."

"And who else?"

Carol thought for a minute. "Chet? The gym is his responsibility. He wouldn't have to pay for the floor, but his gym would be out of business for a while. Maybe our bad guy thought that would hurt his reputation or something."

Molly grinned. "So who does every attack have in common?"

"Chet," Carol answered, her eyes widening.

"But why?" Laura asked. "What's he ever done to deserve such ire?"

Molly shook her head. "I don't know. He hasn't lived in Loch Mallaig very long, and he's only worked here at Castleglen for about a year. We have no idea where he's from and what he left behind when he moved here."

"So we think our bad guy is after Chet, not Rocky." Carol stretched out her legs. "But we have no idea why."

Angus jumped up beside Molly, and she cuddled him. "That's as far as I've gotten."

"Well, I have a question." Laura spread her hands wide. "Do we still think there's a gunman hiding somewhere in this building?"

Carol was quick to answer. "Harvey and I have been talking, and we've decided there isn't."

"Why?" Molly had her own idea here, but she wanted to hear Carol's thoughts.

Carol held up her index finger. "First, it's not logical that there are multiple bad guys skulking around the darkened halls of Castleglen." She held up a second finger. "And there's never been a clue that anyone but Lou has been hiding here. There were several signs of Lou's presence despite the fact that he kept himself hidden for two days. Could there really be a second person completely avoiding notice?"

"So it's someone in our group of guests?" Laura's expression turned thoughtful.

"It's a crime of opportunity." Molly stroked Angus's back. "Someone saw circumstances fall his or her way and took advantage."

"Everything does have that feel," Laura agreed.

"Look!" An excited Trace raced in, Hero at his heels, and pointed to the windows. "It's letting up out there."

Molly smiled. "Told you."

He peered eagerly at the still-gray skies. "I haven't seen blue sky the whole time I've been here."

"Wait and see," Laura told the boy. "It's going to be beautiful."

"Trace." Molly waved to him. "Can you help me?"

He hurried over. "What do you need, Mrs. Ferris?"

"I need to speak with Chet, but I can't really go to him with my bum ankle," Molly explained. "Would you see if he's available for a few minutes? He's probably in his office."

"Sure." He slapped his hands against his knees. "Come on, Angus. You can come with Hero and me."

Angus perked up at the invitation and hopped off the sofa to follow Trace from the room.

In no time, Chet entered the den. Today he wore a tight black sweater that showed off his toned physique. His sweatpants and shoes were very high end, much more stylish and costly than what the usual Loch Mallaig resident wore.

"What can I do for you, Molly?" His face wore its usual pleasant expression. "More crutch lessons?"

"I don't think more lessons will make any difference," Molly said wryly. "Crutches and I will continue to have a contentious relationship as long as we're forced together. No, we want to ask you some questions."

Chet blinked at her unexpected comment.

"Pull up a chair," Laura said. "You might as well be comfortable while we grill you."

Chet eyed the three friends uncertainly.

Carol waved a hand. "Don't worry. We don't suspect you of anything. We know you're not the bad guy."

"You think I'm the target," he said flatly.

"We do," Molly confirmed.

"And you're not surprised," Laura noted.

Chet pulled up a chair. "I've wondered, but I couldn't figure out why."

"That's where we come in." Molly smiled encouragingly. "Where did you live before you moved here?"

"Southern California," he answered. "I was a personal trainer for several movie and TV actors."

"They've got to build those muscles and trim those waists," Laura said.

"And that takes a lot of hard work," Chet replied. "The camera is not kind to any extra pounds."

Molly could imagine him with his pleasant manner encouraging famous people to push through the pain of a strenuous workout. "Did you know any of the movie people here back in Hollywood?"

"Only by name or reputation. I never worked with any of them." He grinned. "It would have been fun to be Matt Bryant's trainer."

Laura leaned forward. "If you had a good business going back there, why did you move away? Or maybe you didn't have a successful business?"

His shoulders squared. "My business was very successful, thank you." He paused, and his air of pride collapsed. "I just don't like talking about why I moved."

The Bakehouse Three waited patiently.

He made a face. "My marriage fell apart about three years ago."

"I'm so sorry," Molly said, a sentiment echoed by her friends.

He shrugged. "An all-too-familiar story. I still haven't really figured out what went wrong."

Adrian, Fergus, Trent, and Harvey entered the den. The foursome got out playing cards and began a game of poker, using sugar packets from the coffee bar as their betting tokens.

Chet eyed them with longing. Molly guessed that he either really liked playing poker or really disliked talking about his marriage. She'd bet it was the latter.

He continued his tale. "Fortunately, Jill and I had no kids, but everything still became awkward. Jill is a personal trainer too, and our work and social lives were very entwined. We even had a couple of clients where I coached the husband and she worked with the wife in their home gym at the same time." He shook his head sullenly. "Then our friends had to choose too, or they felt they did. I have to say for Jill that she was never nasty or accusatory. It might have been easier for me if she had been. Then I could have gotten angry at her and told myself that it wasn't my fault." He appeared lost. "What if it was?"

"Sounds like you simply grew apart," Carol said sympathetically. "It happens."

Chet gave her a small, appreciative smile. "After a while, I got tired of feeling like I was walking on eggshells in LA. And I decided I wanted to do more than help rich people stay in shape. The idea of having my own gym with a full range of services took hold."

"But why here?" Molly asked.

"I wanted something completely different from Southern California. I wanted somewhere that wasn't so expensive, but outdoor life was vibrant. And I wanted a town where I wouldn't bump up against a chain gym or an already established business. Michigan appealed to me, and when I visited the area, I fell in love with Loch Mallaig."

Laura glanced at Molly and Carol. "Some of the reasons the three of us are here."

"But you didn't follow through on your own gym," Molly said.

"I came close," Chet told her. "I had my business plan all worked out. I had the financing arranged on a great piece of property. Everything but signing on the dotted line. Then Fergus approached me about the job here at Castleglen. I realized I'd have all the creative freedom I wanted with none of the headaches and worries of trying to make it on my own. Best of both worlds for me."

Bobby stuck his head in the den door. The poor man looked like he'd barely survived fifteen rounds with the heavyweight champion of the world. The lump on his forehead was angry and both eyes were black. "Hey, Chet," he called. "Trace is fiddling with the free weights."

"By himself?" Chet jumped to his feet and started for the door. At the threshold, he turned back to the women. "Here's a small-world thing for you. My ex, Jill, is dating Adam Lorbetski. Who'd have thought, huh?"

As she watched Chet and Bobby disappear, Molly realized her mouth was hanging open at that revelation. Adam was dating Chet's ex-wife? She remembered her first conversation with Trace at Bread on Arrival. He told her Adam's girlfriend had an ex who bothered her, stalked her. She told Laura and Carol.

Carol pushed the idea aside. "No way is Chet stalking her. She's in California. He's here in Michigan and has been for over a year."

Laura pulled her feet under herself and wrapped her arms around her legs. "I agree with Carol. There must have been someone between Chet and Adam, and he's the guy bugging her."

"Well, whoever he is, he's probably not our troublemaker." Molly shifted her position slightly, growing tired of being laid up.

"Because all kinds of things happened after Adam was out of the picture," Laura said.

"Exactly," Molly agreed. "The ex would have no reason to continue making trouble."

"We still don't have a motive," Carol said. "I don't see one in what Chet told us."

Molly put her hands beneath her head so she didn't feel quite so flat. "They always say it's motive, means, and opportunity. We don't know the motive yet. We know all the crimes were crimes of opportunity. So what about means?"

"The means were whatever was available." Carol stared into the fire contemplatively. "The wastebasket fire took advantage of what was in Chet's office. The bad guy only needed matches, and there are some right here." She indicated the box of extra-long matches resting on the mantel.

"For the broken window, he took advantage of the weights that were lying there," Laura observed.

"But the shootings," Molly said. "They're a different story. Someone wanted to do serious harm. Someone had a gun, so it was premeditated."

Carol sat up straighter as an idea struck. "Does that rule out the California gang? They couldn't have gotten a gun past airport security and onto their plane."

Laura took up the logic thread. "And if one of them had bought a gun since arriving, wouldn't the others have seen that?"

"What about Trent's outfitters shop?" Molly asked. "They all went at the beginning of the storm, and it must have been chaotic with everyone shopping for clothing and gear."

"Trent doesn't sell handguns," Laura said. "Besides, he would have mentioned it if he'd sold a firearm to one of the people trapped in a resort with an active shooter."

"Then that leaves..." Molly let the words trail off, and silence fell as the ramifications of their thinking struck.

Molly glanced at Laura and Carol and saw the same reluctance and uncertainty she felt reflected in their faces. She dropped her good foot to the floor.

"Before I can handle any more conversation with so many upsetting possibilities, I need to make another trip down the hall. Carol, will you hand me my crutches?"

Carol scrambled to her feet and got them.

Laura helped lower Molly's injured foot to the floor, stood, and held out a hand. "Up you get."

Molly took hold and was soon balanced on the crutches. She took a deep breath and swung herself toward the door.

Laura clapped and whistled while Carol called, "You've got this."

Molly wasn't so sure. She was winded by the time she reached the door, but she soldiered on down the empty hall. It was slow going, but she eventually made it after one stop to rest in the hallway chair. When she reached the ladies' room, she got through the swinging door easily . . . but a few minutes later, she was on the other side, staring at the door that opened in, then at the crutches, then back at the door. This would take some maneuvering.

She set one crutch against the wall, steadying herself on the other while she pulled on the door. It felt much heavier than she remembered. She opened it a few inches, but any thought she had of calling for help vanished when the unmistakable strains of the University of Michigan fight song being sung by an enthusiastic crowd came wafting down the hall.

She shook her head. Fergus, a die-hard Wolverine, must have won the poker game and was celebrating with help from the rest of the group.

After more maneuvering, Molly finally got the door wide enough to slip through, though she was constantly aware of the risk of it getting the better of her and knocking her flat. She emerged as the impromptu glee club stampeded to the grand piano in the hall and began singing "Joy to the World" while Adrian played accompaniment.

She watched the scrum of people gathered outside the den door as she slowly made her way toward them. Harvey grabbed Carol and led her in a lively dance step. Chet offered Paula his hand and they joined in. Rocky reached for Greer, who looked horrified and shook her head decisively.

Molly approached the small conference room where she'd found Lou. Reaching this milestone meant she was halfway there.

She was congratulating herself on getting this far when a movement caught her eye.

She gaped in disbelief as the door opened a slit and a hand holding a gun appeared. Her blood went cold. The shooter was taking aim yet again.

21

Her mind reeling, Molly glanced at Chet. A big grin lit his face as he twirled a laughing Paula out and back. What if the shooter missed Chet and struck her? Or any of the others clustered together?

She couldn't let that happen.

The wooden door hid her from the shooter's view. Without hesitating she swung on her crutches toward the conference room and the gun. Just before she reached it, she shifted her weight onto her good foot and lunged, crutch extended like a knight's lance at a jousting tournament. It rammed into the door with all the force she could muster, pushing it shut on the hand holding the gun.

The gun went flying and a cry of pain was nearly lost amid the sound of caroling.

Molly felt herself begin to topple. To keep her balance, she automatically stepped with her bad leg and gave a scream herself. She waved her hands frantically as if that would keep her upright but knew full well she was going down.

"Molly!" Fergus saw her and came running. The singing stopped abruptly as everyone stared, then started toward her too.

Fergus arrived in time to keep her from hitting the floor. Her weight unbalanced him, and they ended in a tangled heap in front of the closed conference room door—where the shooter was now trapped.

"Are you all right?" Fergus asked gently.

"I'm fine." She grabbed his shirt. "The gun, Fergus!" She pointed to where it rested against the wall.

As the remaining singers closed in, Fergus scrambled to his feet and took up position in front of the weapon. No one seemed to notice in their concern for Molly.

"Why didn't you call us for help?" Laura demanded.

"I didn't think you'd hear." Molly tried to rise, so Chet and Trent stepped forward and lifted her to her feet. Carol handed her the lost crutches, and she stuffed them under her arms.

"Did your crutches slip?" Chet examined them after he was certain she was steady. "They shouldn't have."

"They didn't," Molly said. "I used one as a weapon and overbalanced myself."

Everyone turned to stare at her in shock. Then, muffled sobs sounded, and all gazes shot to the door again. Rocky reached to open it.

"First things first," Molly said, gesturing to the gun Fergus was guarding. "The bad guy's not going anywhere."

"What in the world?" Greer joined Fergus and bent to examine the gun as he stepped aside.

"He stuck it out the door. I think he was aiming it at Chet." Molly's stomach pitched as she pictured that shaking hand and the unsteady gun. "I rammed the door with a crutch. I caught him between the door and the jamb." She swallowed. "I think I hurt him."

"Before he hurt anyone else." Greer nodded approval. She pulled on gloves and carefully put the gun in an evidence bag and then in her tote.

Fergus returned to Molly and rested a hand on her shoulder. "You did good, Molly."

"Thank you, Molly." Chet, pale and aware of what she'd done, managed a smile.

Molly blushed.

"Everyone stand back." Greer reached for the conference room door handle. "Here we go."

Disregarding the officer's warning, everyone including Molly leaned forward to see what was beyond the door as Greer opened it.

Lying on the floor and cradling his injured hand to his chest was Bobby Elder, successful real estate agent and failed marksman.

Gasps and exclamations of disbelief filled the air. The real estate agent was no one's idea of a bad guy.

"My wrist." Bobby pouted pathetically at Greer. "My wrist is broken. It hurts so bad."

Greer collected herself and scowled at him. "Bobby Elder, you're under arrest for attempted murder."

"Me?" He tried to act innocent. "Attempted murder? It's all a misunderstanding." With his good arm he pushed himself to sitting.

"It's pretty straightforward to me." Greer patted her tote. "According to Molly, you were holding a gun and aiming it at Chet."

The reality of Bobby's situation hit him, and his eyes went wide and scared.

Molly thought of the time she'd rushed into the locker room hall and found him curled on the floor. She pictured the lump on his forehead, still clearly visible.

"The shooter didn't strike you." Molly now felt stupid for thinking he had. "You ran into the door you'd propped open."

Bobby's eyes darted around wildly, scanning the room behind him and the hallway in front of him as if searching for a hiding place or a way to escape. Neither was available.

"And I felt so sorry for you," Molly added.

There were several murmurs of angry agreement from the crowd of resort guests.

"We found one glove," Greer said. "Where was the other?"

Bobby said nothing.

Molly closed her eyes, the better to remember. "When I came

through the door, I thought he was hurt in his abdomen." She pictured him clutching at his middle. "Now I bet he was stuffing the glove into his waistband."

"Okay," Greer replied. "But what about the gun? He certainly couldn't hide it in those shorts."

Molly stared at Bobby, who wouldn't meet her eye. She sifted through every detail of those moments. "How about this? After he fired, he slid the gun through Chet's open office door, where it went under his desk. When he turned toward the locker room, he was closer to the door than he'd expected. He knocked himself silly running into it and knocked the wedge holding it open free at the same time."

Greer thought about it. "Reasonable crime scene reconstruction."

Molly decided she might as well share the rest of her theory. "When he went to change into his regular clothes, he recovered the gun and set the fire. We were all getting dinner, so he knew no one would see him."

"That's ridiculous," Bobby declared. "It's me, Bobby. You all know me." He furrowed his brow and let his shoulders sag, acting like the injured party being falsely accused, but he was pale and sweaty.

Greer fixed him with a stern look. "You're in big trouble, Bobby. Attempted murder. Assault with a deadly weapon. Destruction of property. Those are just a few of the charges we can level at you. Be thankful Adam didn't die, or the charge would be murder."

"Why, Bobby?" Chet ran a hand through his hair, confused, bewildered. "What did I ever do to you?"

Bobby's mouth fell open, and his scared act fell away to reveal fury. "Are you kidding me? You ruined me!"

Chet recoiled. "I what?"

"You were going to buy that property," Bobby spat. "You were going to build that gym."

Understanding dawned on Chet's features. "And you were my agent." He shook his head. "I get that changing my mind cost you your sales commission, but sales fall through all the time in real estate. That would hardly ruin you, and it certainly isn't motive for trying to kill me."

Multiple emotions flashed across Bobby's face. He pressed his lips together as if trying to keep quiet, knowing that if he started to explain, he might incriminate himself. His cheeks grew scarlet and his cheeks quivered. He glared at Chet and spoke.

"You thought you were so smart with your business plan and your money in hand and your enthusiasm." Scorn laced Bobby's words. "But I saw how to use you. I went to the man who owned the property you wanted and bought it myself. You're familiar with California prices. I could charge you whatever I wanted, and you'd still think it was cheap. You'd have your dream, and I'd make a real killing."

"The ethics of such a deal didn't bother you?" Molly asked. "To say nothing of its legality, which has to be shaky at best."

Bobby sneered at her.

"And then I didn't buy after all," Chet said. "You found yourself stuck with land you didn't have a buyer for, bought at a price you couldn't afford."

Bobby pouted again. "I had to declare bankruptcy."

"Over that one bad move?" Adrian raised his eyebrows. "Why didn't you get a loan to tide you over?"

Bobby flushed and cast a sideways glance at Greer. He cleared his throat. "I'd made a couple of other bad investments, and the bank wouldn't help me. They actually called my loans."

"After how many months of nonpayment?" Adrian asked knowingly.

Bobby ignored the question. He was too busy listing his grievances. "The mortgage company declared my house a forfeiture."

"Again, it begs the question," Adrian said, "after how many months of nonpayment?"

"I was forced to move into a thirdhand trailer. I had to sell my car." The more Bobby talked, the fiercer his anger became.

Molly remembered the luxury SUV Bobby drove around town. *Used* to drive around town. She hadn't seen him in it recently, and now she understood why.

Bobby glared at Chet. "And you? You have it all—good job, good salary, good benefits—and me? I. Have. Nothing!"

The vitriol in his voice chilled Molly to her bones.

Apparently, it had no such effect on Greer. "Chet, do you have another elastic bandage? We probably should wrap his wrist."

"You get it, Chet," Paula said. "I'll wrap it so you don't have to get near him."

"Thank you," Chet said with nearly tangible relief. He cut through the crowd to the gym.

Greer gestured toward the conference room. "Fergus, do you mind if we lock him in here until I can escort him to jail?"

"Not at all," Fergus said with a gimlet eye toward Bobby.

Bobby jerked. "You can't do that."

"Actually, you'll find that I can," Greer said evenly. "We'll give you blankets and a couple of pillows. We'll bring you dinner. We'll escort you to the restroom as needed. But Bobby, get used to being locked in. This is only the beginning."

The sun had barely risen Thursday morning when a snowplow cut its way through the Castleglen parking lot, clearing the way for two police cruisers. While the other guests watched, Greer met Chief

Thomson and Deputy Chief Gillespie at the main resort door and escorted them to the small conference room where Bobby huddled.

"My wrist," Bobby whimpered as he was walked from the room in handcuffs.

"They're expecting us at the medical center." Chief Thomson shook his head. "Elder, what were you thinking?"

Bobby suddenly became deeply interested in his shoes.

Greer stood beside Lou, who was also handcuffed but looked considerably better than Bobby. He'd been allowed a shower in the locker room.

"Don't worry, Uncle Lou." Paula gave him a hug. "I'll come visit you in the big house."

Lou laughed. "I'll be out on bond in a couple of hours. I'll beat you back to California."

"I'm afraid he'll be here in Michigan for a while," Chief Thomson said to Paula. "Things have to be decided under Michigan law, and he'll need to stay in town until they are."

"Fergus, save me a room?" Lou asked.

"Sorry, Lou, but you're banned for life," Fergus answered cheerfully.

Lou shrugged. "Don't blame you. Maybe I'll rent a cabin. I decided I'm going to write a book about the celebrities I've photographed through the years. That will keep me busy for a while." At Rocky's glare, Lou held up a placating hand. "Don't worry. You're one of the nice ones. Do you think Jonathan will represent me when I'm ready to publish?"

Rocky didn't bother to respond.

"Let's go." Chief Thomson urged Bobby forward.

The real estate agent's shoulders slumped, and he stumbled. The idea of prison must be terrifying to him. Molly found herself feeling sorry for him until she remembered how close Adam had come to death. Fortunately, this morning's report had been good. He was awake, aware, and even able to eat and drink a little.

As Bobby made his way down the hall, he spotted Chet through the door of the gym. Chet had his back to them as he showed the deputy chief the carefully covered bullet in the wall. Bobby glared at the unaware man, his fear of the unknown morphing into his much-tended resentment, anger, and bitterness.

The venom in his expression alarmed Molly. Yesterday she, Laura, and Carol had talked about the two Paulas. Today they could discuss the two Bobby Elders.

Chief Thomson paused at the end of the hallway before entering the lobby. "Anderson, as soon as you write your report, you're off duty until next week. You did good work."

Greer glowed as she glanced at Rocky. Hope and uncertainty flew across her face before she could hide them under her cop's stoicism. He grinned and winked. She beamed back at him.

"Now there's a great picture." Lou sighed with regret. Paula opened her mouth, clearly about to scold him, and he held up a hand. "Don't worry. It's just instinct." He followed the assistant chief to the second SUV and climbed in.

"Time to cook." Laura started for the kitchen, stopped and pointed at Molly. "Except for you. Go lie down."

Molly was glad to follow Laura's order. Her foot had ached all through the night, interfering with her sleep. She felt weary and out of sorts. She wanted to go home and climb into her own bed with Angus curled at the bottom, keeping her feet warm.

Fergus smiled at her. "Come on. Let's get you settled." He walked her to the den, where Angus lay with Hero by the fire. After resting her crutches within reach, Fergus draped a blanket over her. "See you at breakfast." He kissed the top of her head, then left for his office.

Paula appeared with a plastic bag of ice and a dish towel, which she arranged on Molly's ankle before returning to the kitchen. Molly smiled at Paula's new confidence as she drifted off. She awoke when people came into the room with plates of food and took seats at the tables.

She knew immediately something was different—something other than the mouthwatering smell of fresh biscuits and bacon. It took her a moment to figure it out.

The distant rumble of the generator was gone. The electricity was back.

After breakfast, the cleanup crew disappeared to do their duty for the last time. Adrian, Rocky, and Trace sat in a corner to call Beverly Scott, the real estate agent who had sold the Bakehouse Three their grand Victorian. Despite their previous agent being arrested for attempted murder, they remained intent on their plan to relocate.

Laura, Carol, and Paula pulled up chairs by Molly. Carol blew on her coffee. "Harvey says we can probably leave before noon. I'm anxious to get home to see how the girls and Pascal survived."

"Girls?" Paula frowned in confusion. "I thought you only had one daughter."

Carol laughed. "We do. I'm talking about our hens. They spent the storm in the garage."

"I'm not sure who had it better," Laura said wryly. "The chickens in a garage or us in a luxury resort with a would-be murderer."

"What are your plans, Paula?" Molly asked.

"I'll leave when Jonathan does, which I expect to be as soon as the airport opens," the young woman answered. "When I get home, I'll tell my parents I'm not interested in the movie business. I'm quitting my job, and I'm going to school to get all the credentials I need to do what I want—which I think is to be an EMT."

Carol patted Paula's hand. "We are so proud of you. If you ever need encouragement or support, you've got a cheering section here in Loch Mallaig who will support you."

Tears shimmered in Paula's eyes. "I may need you, depending on how my parents react."

"Maybe point out what show business did for Uncle Lou," Laura suggested. "He's headed to jail."

Jonathan strode into the den. He all but snarled at Paula, "Are you coming with me or what?"

She jumped to her feet. "I'm all packed. Ready when you are."

"We leave in ten minutes." He started to leave the room, then paused at the door. "I got you a ticket. Coach." The way he said it indicated he was flying first class.

Paula patted her heart after he vanished. "He scares me to death. The drive to the airport is going to be such fun."

After a flurry of hugs, Paula was gone. A moment later, an unexpected group of visitors entered.

"Where's Matt Bryant?" asked Loch Mallaig mayor Tavish Calhoun, who had apparently braved bad roads with his son, Patrick, and his twin grandkids, Ryan and Regan, to catch a movie star before he left town. "I'd like to welcome him to our wonderful town."

While Rocky and Adrian chatted with the Calhouns, Trace eyed the twins. They were his age and a great advertisement for Loch Mallaig. Ryan wasn't as tall as Trace, but he had the cool factor in spades. Regan was beautiful with curly auburn hair hanging down her back and sparkling deep-brown eyes.

Hero had none of his master's shyness and came running to greet the twins. Ryan gave him a quick ear rub, then the dog moved to Regan. She went down on her knees and hugged the wiggling animal.

"Aren't you a cutie?" She laughed as he licked her cheek.

Ryan stuck his hands in the pockets of his ski jacket. "My grandfather says you're moving here."

"So they tell me," Trace replied, indicating his brother and uncle. "I'm still not sure about the whole thing."

Regan smiled at him. Molly could practically sense the boy's knees go weak. "You'll love it here. It's pretty fun."

Ryan seemed to reach some decision. "Some of us kids are going snow camping over the weekend. Do you want to come?"

"Snow camping?" Trace's eyes bugged.

"Yeah," Ryan said, oblivious to the horror in Trace's expression. "My dad and a friend of his are taking about five of us. We snowshoe in and set up camp."

"Camp like . . . in tents and stuff?" Trace asked. When Ryan gave a cheerful affirmative, Trace swallowed visibly. He recognized the offer as an invitation from the in-crowd. "Are you going?" he asked Regan.

"Wouldn't miss it." She beamed at him.

Trace gave her a shy smile, pink creeping into the tips of his ears. "I'd love to go. Let me check with my brother."

The kids moved off, and the Bakehouse Three exchanged knowing glances. Molly watched as Rocky nodded his permission and Trace looked both delighted and terrified. "I think Trent will have another customer soon so Trace can get outfitted for this great adventure."

Laura chuckled. "I hope his thin California blood is tough enough to sleep outside during a Michigan winter."

"My money's on Trace," Carol said. "Or should I say Regan."

Molly shifted her gaze back to the fire, feeling relaxed for the first time since arriving at Castleglen. However, after a few minutes, she started to feel a familiar itch. "We can be up and running at Bread on Arrival by tomorrow morning, can't we?"

"Carol and I can." Laura raised an eyebrow toward Molly's ankle.

"You might do well to rest another few days and let Hamish and Bridget do the heavy lifting for you."

Molly grumbled, but knew better than to argue with Laura.

"We're going to have a busy weekend as people enjoy their release from being snowbound and do their Christmas shopping." Carol withdrew a slip of Castleglen stationery from her pocket. "I've made a list of the things we should definitely have available."

Laura brought out her phone. "Here's my list."

Molly listened as her partners set the day's agenda. The past few days already felt unreal, like an intense dream from which she woke with relief. The twinge from her ankle as she adjusted her position reminded her how real it had been.

But the best was ahead. Christmas at Bread on Arrival was often wild, usually busy, and always wonderful. She couldn't wait.